BLUE

A Novel on the Civil War

BLUE

A Novel on the Civil War

Joe Poindexter

ISBN-10:0991355067

ISBN-13:978-0-9913550-6-8

Freeze Time Media

Cover illustration by Joe and Rose Poindexter

Dedication

*To the memory of one of my heroes, my great uncle —
David Riley Lofland, Bluffton, Arkansas, 24th Regiment,
Company I – Confederate Army.*

Acknowledgment

*My thanks go to my lovely wife Rosalie, who helped me
so much with the book, and my wonderful publisher, Di
Freeze, Freeze Time Media.*

Contents

JOB 19:7

Though I cry, "I've been wrong!" I get no response;
though I call for help, there is no justice.

Chapter 1

Hickory Flats, Tennessee

1860

THE BLOOMING BULL HAD gone through another fence. It was at least the third time in the last two weeks that they had been forced to go after him. David, at first, wondered about a bear, but then he realized that it would take more than one bear to bring down Goliath, the huge, white-faced bull.

"Found him, over here by the salt lick," he heard John Jr. yell.

David started back down the hill where his little brother had located the troublesome bull. The huge male stood there chewing the new spring grass. With one of them on both sides of the bull, they began to drive him back toward the north pasture and the damaged fence.

It took another hour or so to repair the rail fence. Afterwards as the two young men started back home, David glanced over at his little brother. "Be glad to get rid of that stupid bull; can't be one so stubborn in all of Arkansas."

David, the second youngest of four brothers, had been excited about the move to Arkansas for several days after his pa had first mentioned it. However, the twin sisters, Rebecca and Rachel, were not as excited about the move as the boys. Hickory Flats, Tennessee, had been their home during the time they had attended school at the one-room schoolhouse at the edge of town. But now, the children, except for John Jr., were all grown. They all respected their ma and pa and they all realized that a move was something their pa had thought much about.

John Lofland, the husband of Sarah and father of the six children, had asked the entire family to gather outside on the large, front porch that extended across the big, two-story house. The house, unlike a lot of the neighbors' homes, was set on a solid foundation. There were large, stone fireplaces at each end of the home. The home, at one time, belonged to a wealthy farmer and his family. Like many of the earlier upper-class homes, a separate kitchen had been located about thirty feet north of the main structure. It was likely that house slaves had prepared food in the separate kitchen at that time. At some later date, someone had built an attached kitchen on to the house.

Upstairs were two bedrooms. One of the bedrooms was now occupied by David, eighteen, and John, thirteen. Rebecca and Rachel, both nineteen years of age, used the other bedroom. On the main level of the home, outside the parlor, living room, and new kitchen were two bedrooms. The older boys, Wilburn, age twenty-two, and William, twenty, occupied one of the bedrooms while their father John and his wife, Sarah, used the other bedroom.

David loved the home, even if it was in need of some repair. John had acquired the old home from the bank in Selmer. The bank had foreclosed on the home's owner sometime in 1851. That was the same year that John, Sarah, and six children had arrived on the trek from Burnsville, North Carolina. Unfortunately, the youngest child, Joe, had died and was buried during the trip to Tennessee.

David loved to hear his pa's stories about the trip from North Carolina. More than once, John had told the family several stories about their encountering Indians, outlaws, and numerous other problems while on the trip. His favorite story was about some Cherokee Indians that had stolen one of the oxen. John, with one of the accompanying travelers, went after the thieves. According to his pa, the two men caught up with the four Indians that had taken the ox.

"Had a fire, 'bout ready to comist cooking ole Blue," David still remembered his pa saying. "One was stirring the fire. I fired at him and hit him smack in the ear — the ball went rite into the ear hole, clean as a whistle. He fell rite into the fire. Curt hit one rite in the butt. Reckon that smarted. Other two are likely still runnin'; I'd 'spect. Sure ole Blue's glad to see us'uns."

David remembered asking if they buried the dead Indians.

"No way; took ole Blue and headed back to the wagons. We hooked ole Blue up and left afore sunup."

When David thought about the story, he wondered why anyone would mess with his pa. Even today at forty-two years of age, John was over six feet and weighed more than 200 pounds. At only five feet, ten inches, and almost 150 pounds, David wondered if he would ever be as big and muscular as his pa. As he brushed his blond hair over to the side, John began to address the family sitting on the big porch, interrupting his thoughts.

"As you'uns know, we been talkin' 'bout moving agin," he began. "Uncle Seth sent a letter from Arkansas other day. Seth said land over in the middle part of Arkansas is selling fer pennies on the acre. He and Aunt Allie found good land — river bottomland over there. Said 'nother forty acres was fer sale on down aways from him. Seth said they's a small town not fer from him where one can git sugar and flour and other things. Name's Bluffton. Also a cotton gin and grist mill there."

As his pa talked, David noticed that the lightning bugs had now begun to come out. Summer was almost here. He heard a dog barking up near the Nelson's house as John continued to speak.

"Thomas Crittenden, Nelson's son–in–law, has agreed to buy our farm along with some of the furniture. He and the Nelsons will buy all twelve head of cattle and the goats. Course the wolves got one of the goats last night. Since Thomas has been so fair, I throwed the chickens in as well. As part of the bargain, Thomas will give us'uns his team of oxen and wagon. So, we'uns will have two team of oxen and two wagons. When we ready, I'll drive one wagon and Wilburn will handle the other one."

John coughed and then turned and spit off the porch. David heard the bull bawling up near the woods. He hoped that wolves had not arrived again.

"Today, after church, I told the parson that he and the Missus could have anything else that we can't take along," John said. "Your ma has already decided what furniture she wants to take along with clothes, pots and pans, and what food we can carry. As you'uns know, your ma and me already done this once when we come to Tennessee. The trip will be 'bout 250 miles."

David wondered how his pa knew this — maybe from Uncle Seth.

"Now for the important part," John said, quickly slapping his left arm. "Them darn moskitos — hope they's not so bad in Arkansas. We will go to Memphis first — 'bout eighty or ninety mile. There, things change. We will load my wagon, oxen, furniture, and couple barrels of corn on one of the big paddle wheeler boats. I will take the boat down the Mississippi

River to where the Arkansas River empties into the Mississippi River. There near a place called Arkansas Post, the old capital of Arkansas, the boat will turn back north on the Arkansas River. Me and the wagon and goods will go north on the boat to Little Rock. When I get there, I will take the wagon and team to Bluffton. I figure 'bout four or five weeks."

"Pa, why not let one of us boys go with you? We not gonna need no three men with the second wagon," questioned William.

"I've thought it out Bill," John said, looking back at his second oldest son. "I want you three older boys to take care of the womenfolk and make sure all the other goods gets there awright. Seth said it can be rite dangerous going that way. Have to watch out fer robbers and thieves. Ya'll have guns and I'll have a gun."

"Okay, Pa."

"Now with the Lord's help, both the wagons should arrive there 'bout the same time. When you'uns git there, ask around for Seth. He will take you in," he concluded, coughing a couple of times.

"Look, a falling star," said Rachel. "Is that a good sign or a bad sign?"

"Neither," replied Wilburn. "Just a falling star."

"We have enough money as long as we don't run into serious trouble," John stated, looking at Sarah.

David wondered if this new journey would be as exciting as the one that the family had taken while coming to Tennessee. No doubt, if he had his way, he would go with his pa down the river.

"Pa, when we gonna leave?" asked Rebecca.

David knew why she was asking this question. Becky, as they called her, had a young man by the name of Orville who frequently came to call on her. David was aware of the two lovers' relationship because he had discovered the couple in the barn once, rolling in the hay. He had been shocked at what he had seen. Later, David had told William what he had seen.

"Don't dare mention that to Pa — or anyone," William had warned. "He would beat Becky half to death if he found out what happened. Might kill Orville."

David took this to be good advice; however, he would be more observant in the future.

"We will leave a week of Saturday, rain or shine," David heard John answer Becky's question. "I've told Thomas that he kin move in on Sunday — the next day. We outa a home by then."

"Let's be in prayer about our move to Arkansas and to Bluffton," John said, again looking over to Sarah.

Better pray for Becky to, David thought.

"Let's hit the sack — lot to do fer the next week or so," said John as he turned to go back into the house. No one said anything as they all followed him.

"You reckon Arkansas will be anything like Tennessee?" asked Junior as they got into bed.

"Might be little different — remember Arkansas has only been a state few years," replied David.

"You thank they's got more Indians over there?" asked the younger John.

"Probably. Uncle Seth said they's Cherokees over there."

Chapter 2

The Lovers

THE WEEK PASSED QUICKLY as everyone worked hard to meet the departure deadline for leaving the state. There was also little free time for the younger family members. David could tell that Becky was really worried about leaving, especially after informing Orville about the move. He wondered if Rachel, the other twin, knew about Becky's relationship. The busy Sarah, usually humming or singing a church hymn, continued to supervise the storage of items as well as deciding what would be destroyed or given away. The twins also worked hard to assist their mother.

Two days before the Saturday departure, the men began loading the two Conestoga wagons. Wilburn's wagon — or wagon #2, as John had designated it — was loaded first. This wagon would carry the family's clothing; the kitchen items, such as the dishes, pots and pans; the wooden wash tubs and buckets; and four of the caned dining chairs. They would not place the food on the wagon until the morning of departure. All knew that the wolves and bears would love to sample the salted hams, sausage, and bacon.

Sarah supervised the girls as they stored more than a hundred jars of canned vegetables. The question was — could the jars stand the shock of the rocky roads and trails ahead?

The excitement increased as wagon #1, John's wagon, was brought up to be loaded. They had to load this wagon carefully, since the family's furniture — including the four double beds, the dressers, five chairs, and the dining room table — must be transported west.

The men also had to find room for the wooden plows and harrow; John even took the well pulley and the well bucket. All of John's tools, including the axes and cross cut saws, were carefully stored away. Sarah wanted to take the porch swing, but there was not enough room.

Two barrels of field corn were put on board for supplemental food for the oxen. The mule would be tied to wagon #2 and follow the wagon. All the bedding would be left in the house and used to make pallets on the floor for the final two nights. Orville, Becky's boyfriend, came over on the last two days to help, but he and Becky got very little done. After not seeing them for a while, David wondered if the lovers had gone back to the hayloft again.

On Friday, the day before departure, several church members showed up just before lunch with a variety of delicious foods for a going away dinner. They also brought food for the family to take on their trip. Parson Bud Claxton, the newlywed pastor, brought his young wife, Lillie. The Loflands would give the Claxtons anything they could not carry, including one of the hogs.

After they had set up a makeshift table and covered it with food, the parson stepped forward and asked for everyone's attention. David thought, oh no, we may be here a while if he gets wound up.

"Friends and neighbors, we are gathered here today to send our beloved neighbors, the Loflands, on a long journey to Arkansas," the parson addressed the gathered crowd. "We show our appreciation by being here to send them off in Christian love. We mix and share our food. We all will miss them so much. Would you bow with me in prayer as we ask the Lord to keep his hand on the Loflands."

As everyone bowed their heads, David instead stared across the table at Lillie. He had caught her looking at him a few minutes earlier, in rather a sad way. Now, her head was bowed, but David could tell that her shoulders were shaking. Was she crying for me, he thought?

At age nineteen, she was a year older than David. Many people, including David, considered the blonde-haired, petite girl the most attractive girl in the area. Lillie and David had become good friends while attending church together. Actually, it was more serious than that — Lillie was the first girl that David had kissed. They had been in love — and probably were still in love.

As the pastor prayed, David thought of that day two months earlier when Lillie had told him something he hadn't been expecting to hear. On a beautiful Sunday afternoon, the parson had asked her if she wanted to take a buggy ride. Lillie's parents were good friends with the preacher, and Lillie's father was a deacon, so Lillie felt that she should not offend the fifty-two-year-old pastor, who had lost his wife of thirty–one years almost three years before.

The parson, well over six feet tall, was not an attractive man. A large man, his stomach seemed to start near his chest and bow way out before it hung down three or four inches below the belt line. He had a huge head, with hardly any hair on top of it. However, he had a large, healthy beard that extended across his face and down about six inches below his chin. His ears were large and his left eye had a slow twitch that seemed to increase when he got excited. Lillie said that the pastor's eye had really twitched as he talked to her during the buggy ride.

Hearing the pastor say "amen" brought David back to the present. He felt bad, knowing that he hadn't heard any of the prayer, because instead, he was thinking of the parson's wife — the only woman he had ever loved.

He looked up quickly to see Lillie staring at him with her beautiful, green eyes. As people began to eat, he continued to think about what she had told him that day.

"David, he didn't touch me — we just talked," the troubled girl had stated.

"Well, what did you talk about?" David had asked in an astonished manner.

She had told him that the pastor had mentioned that he had been observing her in church for a couple of years. Beyond knowing that she was a good, Christian woman, he admitted to finding her attractive.

"He said that he had prayed about it and felt that I might be the woman to fill the void in his life," Lillie had related to David. He had told her to give what he had said some serious thought, and to pray about it. He also asked her to discuss it with her parents.

As he recalled that conversation, David again glanced at his former girlfriend. She was looking at him, and he saw tears rolling down her pretty face. He knew how she felt inside. He hurt so, for Lillie and for himself.

When she had told him about the conversation with the parson, he knew instantly that her parents would approve of the match — and probably even promote it. After all, the parson owned a small, two-bedroom home, oxen and wagon, pigs and chickens, and a garden. Furthermore, Parson Claxton was well respected in Hickory Flats.

David also knew that Zabel, Lillie's father, had a family of ten, including four daughters. He knew that Zabel would want to marry his daughters off to the best prospects.

"Do you think that it is the Lord's will that I marry the parson?" Lillie had asked, clearly confused about the decision she had to make.

"Lillie, it's hard to know the will of God," had been his response. "I guess you'd have to make that decision yourself. But I know one thing; we love each other! Course the parson probably loves you, but I wonder if you love him?"

He recalled Lillie telling him how mixed up she was. "I have prayed, as mother asked so many times, but I'm still mixed up!" she had said. "I do want to do what God would have me do!"

David had told her he would accept her decision, no matter what it was. As he stole another look in Lillie's direction, he recalled how passionately they had kissed that day before drawing apart and what he had said to her. "Regardless, I will always love you Lillie, and I only want you to be very happy."

David had been heartbroken when Lillie told him of her decision to marry the parson. The marriage had occurred just two weeks ago — and David had not attended.

David tried to shake off his thoughts of Lillie. He talked a little to Ralph Curry, the Lofland's neighbor to the north. Even his heartbreak couldn't stop him from noticing that the meal was delicious — especially the wide variety of desserts brought by the neighbor women.

He glanced up occasionally to look over at Lillie, careful to do so without the pastor seeing him looking at his wife. Once David caught her eyes and she smiled, showing her perfect, white teeth.

When lunch was over, everyone broke up into male groups and female groups. David played a game of horseshoes with Frank Nelson, William, and Wilburn, and then headed around the house toward the outhouse. As he neared the outhouse, he noticed someone behind the smokehouse, to the east. The woman, looking down at the ground, was crying. When he realized it was Lillie, he rushed to her side.

"I'm sorry, David," she said, wiping her eyes.

"Let's step into the smokehouse," he requested, reaching for the doorknob.

Lillie immediately turned and entered the smokehouse, and David followed her. Her tears ran down her face as she silently cried. David walked over to her, put his arms around her, and pulled her close to him.

"Oh, David, I can't stand to see you leave for good," she cried, looking up into his eyes. "May the Lord forgive me, but I think of you every day. I know I will never see you again. I love you so much, but yet, I can't love you. Am I evil?"

"No, you could never be evil," David said, struggling to hold back his own tears. "You just did what other people wanted you to do — and maybe it was right."

Suddenly, Lillie placed her hands on her stomach and bent over. "I may be sick again — I've had some stomach problems."

"Could you be pregnant?" asked David, concerned for Lillie, and yet, hating to think about the idea.

"That's not possible, David," Lillie said as she slowly straightened up and removed her hands from her stomach. "We have never had such relations."

David was instantly relieved, but also surprised. After all, the pastor was a man and Lillie was a beautiful woman.

"Either he can't do it, or he doesn't care for sex," Lillie said, as if she had read his mind. "But he is so good to me, I can't but help admiring and respecting him." She paused and then quietly said, "I have often wondered lately if I even want to live anymore, David."

"Don't ever say that again! Neither God nor I wanna hear that. I'll be out of your life, and there's no doubt, the parson can provide for you much better than I could right now. He is good to you and you are surrounded by Christian people, including your parents," David said, glancing down at the ground.

"David, I would give ten years of my life if I was going to Arkansas with you tomorrow," Lillie said sadly.

David tightened his left arm and hand around Lillie's back and pulled her closer to him. With his right hand, he quickly wiped away his own tear.

"We better go, David," Lillie tearfully said, looking toward the door.

Looking into her beautiful face, David thought, how could the parson keep from touching you?

"Lillie, please allow me to kiss you one last time," he said, looking into her eyes. Without a pause, their open mouths met and their lips compressed tightly and moved back and forth, as if they knew it was their final kiss.

"I love you, Lillie, and I wish you good luck," David said, stepping back and looking toward the door. "Let me leave the smokehouse first, and then you leave in a couple of minutes."

"Good-bye, David," said Lillie, "and God bless you."

As David walked towards the outhouse, he realized that he was no longer so excited about leaving Tennessee. There was no other occasion for him to talk to Lillie the rest of the day, until she and the parson boarded the buggy for home. And then it was only group good-byes. As they drove away, Lillie never looked back at him.

David slept little on Friday night. He could not get the lovely Lillie out of his mind. Why — why had it ended this way? Surely God didn't plan this so he would lose his love. If so, God wasn't fair. He surely knew that Lillie loved him. Was it just to pacify a preacher? By the time he went to sleep, David was mad at the fat preacher and God as well.

Chapter 3

The Trip Begins

EARLY THE NEXT MORNING, the Lofland family resumed the final packing. The bedding and food provisions were stored on the wagons. David was feeling better now as he again thought about the trip. He did notice Becky looking up the road to the east. David thought, no, Becky, neither Orville or Lillie will come.

John said a brief prayer, asking the Lord to keep his hand on the travelers while they moved west. David, still angry with God, did not bow his head. John, Sarah, and Junior climbed into wagon number one. John switched the oxen and the trip was underway. Wagon number two, with Wilburn driving the oxen, had the rest of the family except for William, who was riding the mule. David and his ma sat in the wagon seat with Wilburn. Most of the family members looked back at their old home one last time as the wagons went over the hill to the west.

During the first day out, the Loflands were able to wave good-byes to several neighbors as they passed through familiar territory. They were able to stop for the first night at one of John's cousin's home, who was also a Lofland. After unyoking the oxen and watering them, David and Junior entered Wally Lofland's small home, where people were sitting on everything including the floor.

The adults ate at the table while the younger members of the family ate where they had been sitting. After supper, most of the group found a seat on the long front porch. The men listened as Wally told John about a shortcut to Bolivar.

"It will be least eight to ten miles shorter to Memphis — almost a full day with oxen," explained Wally. "Maybe some Cherokees, but no danger. They's stragglers from the Cherokee Trail when Jackson moved 'em west to Arkansas and the territory. Now they'al steal, so mind your livestock and womenfolk."

"They'al do 'bout what they want, as I recall," laughed John. "But ya still have to feel sorry for 'em. I'll never forget when the main body moved from North Carolina, Georgia, and Tennessee. They calling it the 'Trail of Tears' now, and I can see why. Those poor devils were starving to death. You'd find dead men, women, and young all 'long the trail. Don't know how they survived — graves everywhere. I remember an old woman, probably close to seventy years, couldn't keep up and they just left her behind. Wolves ate several of the old ones. You can say what you want to 'bout the Indians, but this was their country first. Jackson and Van Buren stole their lands and sent 'em packing. Lots of northerners talk about the evils of slavery, but they say nothing 'bout the way we's treated the Indians — it's disgraceful." David and William agreed with their pa while Wilburn and Junior disagreed.

As the oxen plodded on west, David thought again about Lillie — gosh, he loved her. He remembered one of the last times that he had gone over to the Mashburn home to see Lillie. As he recalled, it was shortly before she told him about the parson's proposal. Lillie, her mom, and Milli, the oldest of her three younger sisters, had been canning tomatoes. He remembered how attractive Lillie looked in her older, cotton, everyday dress. She was moving quickly, back and forth in the kitchen, checking on everything. It was obvious that she, not her ma, was in charge of the canning project. Yet, she continued to visit and laugh in her characteristic, cheerful manner.

It was obvious that Milli idolized her. Millie had a disposition similar to her older sister. She had a friendly, open personality; yet, there was a seriousness about her. David remembered Lillie asking him if he would help her carry the jars of tomatoes down to the root cellar, located about thirty feet north of the Mashburn home. He carried a box containing twelve quart jars of tomatoes, while Lillie carried four quarts, one under each arm, and one in each hand. Once in the damp cellar, he had carefully stacked the jars of tomatoes on the wooden shelves. After the last jar had been placed on the upper shelf, David had looked down to see Lillie looking at him. He turned to face her and she reached out her arms and quickly pulled him close to her.

"David, I want you to know that I love you so much," she had said, looking up into his eyes.

Then she had passionately kissed him. He had never been so aroused by his lovely friend. Maybe it had been good that Milli arrived at the cellar door with the last of the tomato jars.

David was suddenly awakened from his past thoughts, when a huge, buck deer bolted out of the timber and in front of the wagon.

Chapter 4

Cherokees

THE SECOND DAY WAS a beautiful, summer day. A light, southern breeze gently pushed a few scattered clouds. It was warm but comfortable. The two wagons had been on the old road an hour or so by eight a.m. Even the slow-moving ox teams seemed to be delighted to be moving west.

"Looks like Becky has been crying; is she all right?" David asked his ma.

"Son, she has yet to get over Orville. Your pa and me think it was for the best. We doubted that Orville could have provided for her. As your pa says, Orville's missing some teeth in his saw blade. Besides, he could have come with us but he didn't want to leave his ma and pa. That tells you something. A man has to make hard decisions about life. And a man's wife comes before his folks — and I would tell you the same thing if you were 'bout to marry."

As he listened to his ma, David thought, I would've put Lillie over my folks if I had a chance to marry her. He missed the last part of his ma's comments as he thought of his beautiful friend with tears moving down her face.

"Ma, we ever have a divorce in our family or someone who married a divorced person?"

"Lands, what a question, David. No, we believe when one marries, they do it as the Bible says — for better or for worse.

19

To marry a divorced person is to commit adultery — that's scriptural. Parson preached on that subject jest 'bout two weeks ago — don't you 'member?"

"Yeah, think I recall now," replied David. He wondered what Lillie thought about that sermon.

"You talking 'bout divorce; that's one of the reasons we didn't want Becky to marry that lamebrain. We afraid it would wind up in divorce," his ma responded.

David noticed that William, on the mule, had ridden back to talk to John in the front wagon. After a short conversation, he rode on back to speak with David and his ma.

"We gonna pass some Indians up head. Pa said to remind you." William said, and then turned the mule and started back up in front of the lead wagon. Shortly, the wagons reached two old log cabins. Both were near falling down. The roofs were patched with old boards, and the window openings had boards across the openings. Except for a hog pen with two hogs, they saw no livestock around the old homes. On a small porch of the second cabin, an old man and an old woman sat staring at the wagons. They were dressed in rags. With so little clothing, it was easy to tell that the two old people were thin and emaciated.

David slowed the wagon and then stopped the ox team. From the back of the wagon, Rachel asked why they were stopping, but she got no answer. David leaped to the ground and quickly walked around to the back of the wagon.

"Rachel, hand me one of the hams," he said as he looked inside the wagon.

"Why?" Becky asked, reaching for one of the hams. David took it without answering and started up toward the older people.

As he neared the couple, the old man slowly stood up. "Low."

"I have a ham for you, if you will take it?" said David, looking at the old couple. The old man reached out, took the ham, and bowed his head. David turned, walked back to the wagon, climbed up and took his seat.

"That was a Christian thing to do, David," said Sarah, looking at him with admiration. "I'm proud of you."

As the oxen began to move on, David glanced back toward the old people. Four or five other Indians came out of the house to question the old man. Slowly he put up his hand, as if to wave.

"We need to pray for people who have been hurt so bad," said Sarah. "God will help them."

"Think so? Does God help us when we have got a raw deal?" asked David.

"Why, David, you know so; look how he has blessed us so."

"Ma, didn't brother Joe die on the trip to Tennessee?"

"Yes, he did, but that was the Lord's will," answered his ma.

"Well, Ma, couldn't it be God's will that the Indians are poor and starving? Look at the Cherokee Trail and how many starved and died. Wasn't anyone praying?" argued David.

"David, that's sacrilegious talk; are you losing your faith?" his ma said, glaring at him.

"No, but I don't understand sometimes," said David.

"Well, we can't understand all things," responded his mother. "We just have to keep faith."

Just then, Becky came up to tell her mother that she was sick to her stomach. David was still wondering if God was concerned about mankind. He thought again of Lillie. Was God rewarding the pastor at the expense of Lillie and him? David thought, no doubt, the fat preacher is probably thinking that God blessed him with a beautiful virgin — and yet, Lillie was still in love with him.

Chapter 5

The Auction

AFTER PASSING THROUGH BOLIVAR, the Loflands noticed other Conestoga wagons on the road moving west.

"Pa, all these wagons going to Arkansas?" asked John Jr., who had now moved up to wagon number one to ride with his father.

"Naw, most are going on west, some toward California. We won't see many after we cross the Mississippi River and travel toward Little Rock."

After another week, the travelers were nearing the outskirts of Memphis. Except for John, none of the group had ever been to a city that size. Memphis had become a major port on the Mississippi River. With directions, the Loflands were able to stay on the major road leading to the river docks and the ferry.

Once they had reached the docking area, John suggested they tie up the oxen and visit that part of Memphis. All wanted to see the steamboats and river traffic, so they made a stop near the ferry landing. By then, most of the party had already begun to think about the family splitting up for the rest of the trip. They remembered that John would be going south on the river, while the others would use the ferry to cross over to Arkansas and travel on without him. As the group strolled down the river road, they came to a corner where many people were moving around a large building.

"It's an auction. Let's go in; we might find something," John said as they drew closer.

"It's a slave auction," Wilburn stated, stopping and turning back to the group. "Do we go in?"

"Well, they have other things," answered John. "Let's go in."

"Me and the girls are not going in," said Sarah as she read the notice on the wall. On a large handbill tacked on the door of the building was a picture of a black male with a small loincloth wrapped around his lower waist. By then, David had reached the notice posted on the wall and read it.

FORREST'S SLAVE AUCTION
SATURDAY MERCHANDISE:
Twelve black males — 12-35 years – prime field hands
Four black males — 36-50 years – prime field hands
Five black males — 51-60 years – assorted
Two Mulatto wenches — 12-20 years – breeding stock
Six African wenches — 20-30 years – new
OTHER MERCHANDISE:
2 milk cows
1 gray mare and colt
1 pair of oxen and yoke
2 ox carts
1 60-gallon soap kettle
3 scythes and cradles
Bullet mold and powder horn
40 gallon of sorghum molasses
4 head of foxhounds
Terms of sale — Cash in hand or note to draw 4% interest.
Proprietor: — Mr. Nathan Bedford Forrest
Memphis, Tennessee

After David had read the entire advertisement, he thought, Mr. Nathan Bedford Forrest must be a wealthy man.

"Might as well go in; might find something," repeated John as he looked at his four sons.

Junior was surprised that he was allowed to go into the auction. It was a crowded arena, much like the sale barn in Selmer, with seats all around a small, open area where the merchandise and goods were displayed. Over to one side was a gate where livestock could be led through to the arena. Across the arena floor were two more doors.

Down at the far end of the huge room was a large stack of a variety of goods. David could see barrels of goods, spinning wheels, a plow with wooden moldboards, numerous jugs, and a variety of foods, mainly salted hams and packaged items.

In the center of the huge barn was an elevated platform. On it were four men, one of whom seemed to be doing some writing. Two of the men were there to move merchandise upon the platform. The fourth man was the auctioneer, a smaller man with a loud voice. He spoke through a bullhorn that broadcast his voice into every part of the facility. The auctioneer must have been already working for some time, since one of the men on the platform had brought him a drink of water. After taking the drink, the auctioneer put the conical device to his mouth.

"If you have received a bid, please report to the table, to the left of the platform, and the sale can be completed. Remember, we prefer cash in hand. Also, we have cider, alcoholic drinks, and cookies off to my right. Enjoy some nourishment before you leave today."

The five Loflands had moved up to where a large number of men were standing around the big platform.

"Be careful about removing your hat; ya might bid on something," said John as he smiled at the boys. The boys laughed. The auctioneer had taken another drink and was ready to continue. "Now, for our major items of sale,"

David noticed ten or twelve black males and females come out of one of the doors behind the platform. Chained together, they were led by a large, man who apparently worked for the sale barn. David was shocked when he noticed that the black women had no clothing above the waist. He glanced towards his older brothers. They too seemed to be primarily sizing up the females.

No one said anything as the group moved to the steps that led up to the platform. The first black to be led up to the auctioneer was a slender male. He also had nothing on but a loincloth. The auctioneer turned to look at the young male and then back to the crowd below him.

"Our first item of the day is a late-teenage negro who comes from New Orleans. You might notice that he is quite muscled up and sound of limb. You will see no marks or deformities that might devalue the sale." The auctioneer reached over and widely parted the black man's lips. "The slave also has sound teeth — something the buyer must always consider. His feet are sound. This is a prime field hand — a hand that will reimburse his costs many times because of his young age."

Observing a slave auction for the first time, David felt some sympathy for the young slave. He had a family — maybe a big family back someplace in Africa. He didn't volunteer to come to America to become a slave. David thought about what it would be like if he had been captured here and sent to another country as a slave. He could not take his eyes off of the young man. The slave's expression was not so much one of fear as astonishment. No doubt, he had never imagined a place so different from his own homeland.

David was sure that the young black had no idea what was

taking place or where he would be going. By then, the auctioneer had opened the bid at 300 dollars. As he glanced around and accepted the changing bids, he talked faster and faster. David looked back to the men that had gathered to watch the sale. The interested bidders would only nod their acceptance of the bid. The bid price rose rapidly as the different men seemed determined to purchase the young black. The auctioneer finally slowed his speaking.

We have a bid of 700 dollars — this slave is worth 900. Okay, 750," as he looked back to a former bidder, "750, 750, 750, sold for 750 to Mr. Stephen Wainwright."

David watched as the slave, held by his arm, was led down the steps of the platform and over to a man who was apparently representing Mr. Wainwright. The auctioneer put the horn to his mouth again.

"Our next item is an eighteen-year-old Mulatto wench. She was purchased from a Jackson, Mississippi, plantation only last week."

By that time, the lighter-colored female had reached the top step of the platform. She, like the male, had on only a loincloth. Whistles and comments were made as the slave reached the auctioneer. David, looking at the young slave, thought, gosh, she's attractive.

"Look at those boobs," he heard a man behind him say.

"This wench can be used for childbearing for years to come," the auctioneer began, reading the crowd's reaction. "The owner may even want to slip out and check on this wench." The men who were watching laughed. "This wench could be a house slave or a field hand, so you can't go wrong. Another thing — she speaks pretty good English after serving on a Mississippi plantation. Now, this wench also has a young pickaninny, maybe four-years-old."

David thought, if she is eighteen, she was only fourteen when she gave birth.

"We will sell the wench and the pickaninny together, or we will sell them separate," the auctioneer continued. "If you want to bid on the twosome, would you hold up your hand?"

David looked around the crowd. Three or four hands were raised. The little girl, almost white looking, had been brought upon the platform. She quickly moved over by her mother and put her arms around her mother's legs.

"The opening bid for both the young and older wenches is 500 dollars. However, if we perceive the final bid too low, we will sell them separately. Okay —500, 500, 600, 650, 700, 750, 800. We are at 800, 800 — 900, 950, 1000 dollars. They are worth far more than that. Again, 1,000, 1,100, 1,200."

David noticed that only two men remained in the bidding. He silently hoped that the men would take the bid higher.

"Again 1,200, 1,300, 1,400 — 1,400 once, 1,400 twice, both wenches are sold to Mr. Tony Miller for 1,400 dollars."

"Thank God," said David aloud. He was sure that the young, attractive black woman had tears in her eyes as she moved down the steps with her daughter.

Chapter 6

The Ferry

"WE HAD BETTER GO; time running short," said John as he turned to his boys.

The five men moved back through the crowd and toward the large, open door. Turning to the left, they began walking south toward the wagons that were parked down the street. In the distance, they could see Rachel and Becky sitting in the seat of the front wagon. When they had reached the wagons, John turned once again to address his family.

"The docking area is down the street on the left, right where the big paddle wheeler is. The ferry is supposed to be on down 'bout another half mile. We'll go on down and see when we can load my team of oxen and wagon, and then we'll see when the ferry leaves across the river."

They moved onto the dock area, and John went into the office facility to talk to the dock manager. Once he had been directed to the manager, a husky, dark-complexioned man, he produced the letter stating that he could board the boat on Thursday, May 10. After some questions, the manager stated that everything was in order, but the wagon and oxen could not be loaded before 2 p.m.

"Well, reckon we got time to get a wagon on the ferry?"

"Yeah, plenty of time, just make sure you are here — we have reserved space for you," stated the man, looking north toward the ferry dock.

Fifteen minutes later, the family reached the ferry service dock. Again, John walked over to the service office. A large, black man was behind the counter, looking out the window.

"You in charge?"

"Naw; I's de ferry man myself. Boss man over der." He pointed to another man who was sorting through a stack of papers.

"Excuse me, sur. You in charge of the ferry?" John asked as he looked at the papers the man was shuffling. The man, concentrating on counting pages, didn't look up, but nodded, indicating that he was the manager. "Reckon how long it will be till we can get ox and wagon across the river?"

"Be ten minutes and two dollars," he said, still looking down.

John, worried about missing his boat, immediately reached for his wallet, pulled out two dollars, and laid them on the table.

The man finished his business, looked at John, and then out to the wagons. "Wanna insure 'em?"

"Don't know what you mean," replied John, a puzzled look on his face.

"For one more dollar, we will insure your freight," the man quickly responded. "Pay you the cost of your freight if it is damaged or destroyed on the crossing."

"Guess not," replied John as he watched the man put the dollars in a box. "We need to save costs."

The man stepped out on the dock and blew a whistle. The black man John had talked to earlier approached and reported to the manager.

"Yes, sur?"

"Moses, this gentleman has a wagon, a team of oxen, and a family that needs to go across. When can you be ready?"

The Negro looked at John and stuck out his right hand. "I's Moses; I see'd you before."

"Howdy. We need to board soon as possible, 'cause I have to leave on the paddle wheeler by two," John said, looking at the black man.

"Sur, we cleaning manure from de ferry but ya can pull your wagon up on de ferry dock — rit over der." Moses pointed back north to the dock.

"Thanks," John said, glancing back in the direction the man had pointed. Then he walked back outside to Wilburn's wagon.

"Wilburn, pull the wagon on down to that rock post and then left up on the loading dock. Shouldn't be long."

At Wilburn's command, the oxen began to move toward the dock. John followed on foot. Over the next fifteen minutes, the family members took turns hugging John. Sarah had tears in her eyes after hugging her husband.

"Please be careful, John. Keep your gun handy. We will pray for you."

David wondered if anyone had prayed for the slave girl and her small child back at the auction. Did God not know about the slave girl? Would he really take care of John and the rest of the family?

After they said their good-byes and dried their tears, Wilburn led the yoke of oxen and wagon out onto the ferry. Six other men would ride the ferry across the Mississippi River. Two of the men had saddled horses that would also cross. The docking ropes were soon untied and the ferry began to move out into the main river channel. All the family members waved back to John, who anxiously watched from the dock. Shortly, he turned and walked back to his wagon.

The ferry reached the west side of the river in about thirty minutes. The only family member that had a problem with the crossing was Becky, who was sick once again. Moses, the ferry operator, reminded her that a lot of passengers got sick while crossing the big river.

After disembarking, Wilburn pulled the wagon over to the Arkansas docking office and went into the office to check on directions. He was surprised to find that a lady was in charge on the Arkansas side.

"Ma'am, we on the way to Little Rock and then on east of Little Rock; which road do we take?"

"Only one road to Little Rock, and it's bad in places," the lady replied curtly. They's several creeks and one river to cross, but we had no rain, so you can probably make it okay. Better be ready; they's some bad folks between here and Little Rock." The woman was looking out the window at the waiting family.

"Are there any more wagons going toward Little Rock that we could go with?" asked Wilburn, looking concerned.

"Not right now; if you wait a few days, some may come," replied the woman. "May through August is our biggest months. If you want to wait, they's a good camp area 'bout a mile — water there, probably safe as you will find on this side. Course lota folks don't realize that along the river is the most dangerous place. Thieves and cutthroats prey on river traffic 'cause that is where the wealthy is."

Wilburn immediately thought about his pa. He also knew that both of the family parties were on a schedule. They could not delay for several days.

"Ma'am, reckon we'll use the camping place tonight and move on tomorrow." He turned and walked out the door of the office and back toward his waiting family.

Chapter 7

Pine Bluff

AFTER LEAVING THE FERRY dock, John went back to his wagon, turned the ox team around, and moved back south to the large boating dock. By then, several people had gathered, some to board the large paddle wheeler, some to express good-byes, and some to watch all the activity. John directed the oxen to a sign pointing to the freight-loading area.

He saw people from all backgrounds, nicely dressed men and women, working class people, and a few people who looked poor. Over to one side were several Negroes, obviously slaves, carefully watched by two armed, husky, white men. John wondered if the same slaves had been purchased earlier that day at Forrest's Slave Auction.

After a delay of an hour or so, John was given instructions to drive his ox team and wagon onto the ramp leading to the lower level of the huge ship. The oxen, at first reluctant, finally moved onto the ramp over the water where a loud, inpatient man met them.

"You Benson?" shouted a man who was looking at a piece of paper.

"No, I'm Lofland," replied John, looking unsure.

"Well, don't stand there; bring 'em on. We don't have all day."

John switched the oxen and they moved down the ramp and onto the ship.

"Take 'em down to the end," yelled a second man.

John directed the oxen down toward the stern of the ship, where a series of stalls were provided for different freight. A black man was in the stall marked 11–B.

"Right's here, Right's here," the black man said, pointing at the proper stall.

John directed the oxen in a huge turn, causing them to enter the stall squarely.

"Wish all'uns could han'le oxen like ya, sur," said the young black man.

"Thanks," John said, getting down from the wagon and moving up to the front of the stall. There he attached a rope from the oxen yoke ring to a heavy metal crosspiece.

"Yo movin' to Nir Orlens?" asked the black man.

"No, going up toward Little Rock," replied John.

"Good, cause we ain't going to Nir Orlens," he said, smiling."

"Will everything be awright here on the wagon?" John asked, looking at the Negro.

"Will till you git off'in da ship," the young black said, and then moved over to the next stall where a man with four cows waited.

John looked around and finally decided to stay on the lower level of the ship so he could watch his family's furniture. The voyage down the river was comfortable enough, except for twice when the ship scraped on a couple of sandbars, and then abruptly slowed down, causing the passengers to travel on a few feet.

The ship approached the confluence of the Arkansas River within three hours. With a couple of blasts from the ship's horns, the old steamer slowly made the sharp turn to the right and into the Arkansas River channel. Those in the front of the ship could now see the town of Arkansas Post, the original capital of Arkansas. Again, there were two long, loud blasts from the ship's horns, probably an alert to the people preparing to board at the Post's smaller dock. The steersman did a good job bringing the big steamship into the docking area. Lines were quickly thrown ashore to secure the paddle wheeler.

John had moved up toward the helm of the ship to watch the proceedings. This time, only a gangplank was extended out to the ship. The group of slaves and their overseers left the ship first. Four or five other people also left the ship, including a well-dressed man and a smartly dressed woman. John wondered if the couple might be wealthy plantation owners that lived in the Delta.

Three men boarded the ship. One carried a box and an impressive looking carpetbag. Probably a peddler, thought John. Then six barrels of some content were wheeled out and onto the ship. Finally, two teams of oxen were brought on board. Once again, there were two loud blasts from the ship's horns. Dockmen were already removing the tie lines.

"How long to Little Rock?" John asked a man who had been standing nearby watching the activity.

"Reckon 'bout six and a half hours, unless we hit sandbars. Probably hit one or two; 'member one time it took a whole day, 'cause the river was down."

"Thanks," John said, moving back to stall 11–B. A man was standing near the stall, curiously looking over the Lofland furnishings.

"Need something?" John asked, approaching the stranger.

The man quickly glanced at John, looking surprised. "Naw, just admiring your furniture. You coming or going?"

"I'm going to Little Rock and then on overland fer a while. How 'bout you?"

"Gitting off at the Bluff. Live there," he said, spitting over the side of the ship, and then looked back at John. "By yourself?"

"Yeah, family's coming on another wagon by land," John replied, and then thought that he should not have told the man that he was alone.

"Well, good luck," the man said, moving on back toward the front of the boat.

John again heard the ship's loud whistle blasts. He looked over his family's possessions, and then moved over to look at the east river bank. A couple of young boys with fishing poles were watching the ship. One of the boys pumped his arm up and down. The helmsman responded with two more blasts of the ship's horn. Both boys waved vigorously at the passengers, and most of them waved back.

John wanted to go up on the upper deck and look around the steamboat; however, he was worried about his family's possessions. He wondered how the family was doing. Were they safe and well? He recalled that Becky had been sick at her stomach several times, and dysentery had killed several who lived around Hickory Flats. He sure missed his family, especially his love, Sarah. But he knew that Wilburn and the other boys were very dependable. After all, Wilburn was even marriage age, but he hadn't found the right one, yet. He was a mature one, all right.

John continued to observe the Arkansas Delta, as the big ship moved further north. The river bottomland along the two rivers appeared to be rich, fertile, and deep. John hoped that the land near Bluffton would be similar to these fertile bottomlands. About an hour later, the ship's horns went off again, this time with three loud blasts. The alert indicated that the ship was nearing a dock area.

John leaned over the four-foot railing to look to the north.

He saw scattered homes, mostly shanties, on both sides of the river. He noticed that they had not passed a large home or plantation for a long time. Then someone mentioned that the ship was approaching the town of Pine Bluff. The activity increased on the ship as people began preparing luggage for departure. Soon, after two more loud blasts from the ship's horns, the big paddle wheeler eased into an unimpressive dock. Dockworkers arrived after a brief time and began securing the big ship. Again there were several curious onlookers on the dock, with most appearing to be poor folk.

A man from the Pine Bluff port authority soon arrived at the lower level of the ship, where John continued to watch cargo being unloaded. The man, with a second man following, stopped in front of John.

"You also going on to Little Rock?"

"Yes, sur. How much further?" asked John.

"Hate to tell you this, but we's got a serious problem up ahead. The river is way down 'bout ten miles upstream, even sandbars showing. It has been so dry this spring, up river, that the river is just too shallow to navigate upstream. Two year ago, we had a wheeler stuck in a sandbar for over a week and it may be that bad now. But both you men have good cargo on board. We will allow you to get off here at Pine Bluff with a reimbursement of three dollars, or you can wait here — could be a week, or two, or more, to see if the river water will rise due to rain up the river. We feel some responsibility for this."

The official glanced back at the other man that had followed him.

"Well, I will get off and wait for a few days. My family's following me, so they may catch me here at Pine Bluff."

"Fine. What about you, sur?" the official said, looking at John.

"If it might be two weeks or more, I believe I will take reimbursement and git off here," replied John. "I've got family coming overland from Memphis to Little Rock."

"You can go ahead and unload your ox and wagon shortly," the official said to John as he opened his wallet and returned three dollars to him. "Good luck."

With those words, he quickly walked over to the next stall.

Chapter 8

The Rest Stop

JOHN DIRECTED THE OXEN through the small crowd and on to the main part of town. The town was definitely no Memphis. For the most part, the houses and businesses were small and unattended. The streets were very rough. He noticed that the local people were not dressed well. He saw several other wagons, some pulled by mules, and some pulled by oxen.

As his wagon slowly moved down the street, John noticed a dry goods store at the end of the block. Several men were sitting on a long bench in front of the store, visiting. Needing some advice as to which road to take to Little Rock, John decided to pull his wagon over, park it under a large oak tree, and get some directions.

He tied up the team, stepped down from the wagon, and started back to the store. Two other wagons had to pass before John could cross the dusty street.

"Hello," called out a couple of the men as he approached the store. One of them, a tall, thin-faced man with a long beard, reached out his hand to John.

"Bet your're a visitor. I'm Ben Shiller; sit down a spell," the man said with a smile.

"John Lofland, from Tennessee. Think I will rest a spell," said John, extending his hand toward the friendly gentleman.

"Where you headed, John?" asked a smaller, bald-headed man seated on the bench.

"Going to Bluffton. Ya'll know which road I'm to take?" John asked, but noticed blank looks on most of their faces.

A couple of the men looked at each other and shrugged.

"Know any other town close to it?" asked a well-dressed man standing near the door of the store."

"Well, not rite off. Know it's 'bout seventy or eighty mile west of Little Rock," replied John, realizing he should have gotten more information about the area from Seth. His brother had mentioned a larger town, if he could remember its name. "Som'in like Dandridge, Danton," he said, glancing around at the men.

"Danville?" interrupted the better-dressed gentleman.

"That's it; Danville. You know of Danville?" asked John.

"Yeah, not far from Dardanelle. Continue on for 'bout a mile, and you'll come to a crossroads. Left goes to Princeton. Take the right road going north at the crossroads. That road will go to Little Rock. Once there," the man said, looking back to John's wagon, "you'll have to go back west ag'in. From there, git some more advice."

"You say go to the crossroads and take the road to the right?" questioned John, looking at the man.

"That's it," replied the speaker.

"Is they a good place to camp for the night round here?" asked John, looking around at the men.

"If'in it was me, I'd just camp near the crossroads," offered a man with tobacco juice on his beard. "Then you could be on your way come morning."

"Believe I will. Thanks men."

"Good luck," one of the men said as John walked back to the wagon. It was at least two miles to the crossroads that the men had told him about. The road to the junction was lined with trees, mostly pine, and cedar, with an occasional hardwood. John could see no homes anywhere in the area. He drove the oxen to the crossroads and then turned them on the road to the right. This road looked to be less traveled than the road leading to Princeton.

Apparently, not a lot of people traveled on to Little Rock, John thought. As he moved further from Pine Bluff, he began to look for a suitable place to camp. The sun was setting in the west and the tall pine trees shielded much of the lower rays of sunlight. It would be dark in an hour. As John scanned both sides of the road for a camping place, he noticed a small clearing off to the right side of the road.

"This ought to do," he muttered to the oxen. With no ditch by the road, he was able to ease the oxen up a slight grade and on to the small clearing. He directed the oxen back to the trees at the far end, and as he pulled on the reins to stop them, he saw some stacked, flat rocks. Then he noticed that the rock piles were placed in a rectangular fashion, and he saw a pile of larger, native rock. Hmm, an old home place, and what's left of the chimney, he thought. In less than a half-hour, he had a good fire going within a circle made from the old, home rocks. He wondered who had lived there and why they had left.

The chopped potatoes and warmed-over ham were delicious. He wished that he had some of Sarah's yeast bread to go with it. Even more, he wished Sarah were there to share his bed on the ground near the wagon. He missed Sarah and the family; yet, he was sure that the family's future would be even brighter in Arkansas.

He finished his coffee and went to the wagon to get corn for the oxen. After feeding them from the wooden bucket, he sat down between the wagon and fire on one of the large, flat rocks. He again thought about his family and then silently prayed for their safety. He hoped that they were a long way toward Little Rock.

Later, as he sat lazily gazing into the flickering fire, he heard something.

"You in bed?" a voice said.

John quickly looked up, paused, and said, "No, come on up."

He looked toward the road in the direction of the voice and saw two figures moving toward the fire. As the two men got closer, John thought he had seen them somewhere recently. He was sure about the man on the left. He was the man that had been looking at John's wagonload of furniture on the paddle wheeler. As the men moved closer, he saw that the second stranger was the well-dressed man from the dry goods store in Pine Bluff.

"Want some coffee?" asked John, starting to reach for the coffee pot.

"No. We want more than that!" Before the speaker finished the sentence, John felt a big hand come around from behind and grab his hair. Out of the corner of his right eye, he saw the knife come around from the other side of his head. Then he felt the knife plunge into and rip across his throat. He felt nothing after that.

"That do it?" questioned the assailant, who crawled out from under the wagon.

"He never knew what happened," replied the well-dressed man. Then he turned to the man who had come with him. "Take his wagon on to the barn, go through it, and remove any names. Could be some money. Jake, you search him good and remove any letters, papers, and money. I'm going back home. You go with Ben to the barn. The county sale is Saturday. We will auction off all his property, including the ox team and wagon. See ya'll tomorrow at the store."

Neither man said a word as the storeowner turned and walked back to his wagon down the road. Very quickly, the diverse, nocturnal animals in the area picked up the smell of fresh blood. By morning it would be hard to recognize the lone stranger found murdered on the county line road.

Chapter 9

Squatters

AFTER CAMPING THE FIRST night near the river, Wilburn and Sarah got the family up early. Sarah had a delicious breakfast of potatoes, sausage, and bread, along with her usual strong coffee. Before the family left their seats around the campfire, Sarah opened the old Bible. The family devotion occurred every day in the Lofland family. It was usually in the evenings, sometimes by candlelight.

However, now on the road, the family usually traveled until dark. Sarah had concluded that now it would be best to have the devotion after breakfast. She opened the Bible to the book of Job. She began to read through chapter three about all the problems that Job had experienced — yet he maintained that he was a righteous man. Job questioned why God continued to bring more and more trouble on him. It got so bad that he even wanted to die. After Sarah finished the Scripture, she looked around at the gathered family.

"This reading is hard to understand, because we know God loves us. And in the end, God will restore Job's family and possessions. That shows that God loves us. We must always remember that, regardless of the trouble that we have in our life. Fortunately, we have seen little trouble."

Sarah bowed her head and prayed for the family. She

also prayed for John, her beloved husband. She had thought about him often since they departed yesterday at the ferry dock.

"Girls, help me with the dishes, pots, and pans," Sarah said as she laid the Bible down on the wagon.

Wilburn and William put the heavy yoke on the oxen and hooked them to the big wagon. Then, Wilburn looked at David.

"You take the mule today, stay a quarter or so in front, and let us know about any trouble spots, 'specially creeks and rough places. Take one of the muskets and stay alert."

"Sure," said David as he walked over to the mule.

Within half an hour, the party was on the road again, moving toward Little Rock. David, on the old, gray mule, was out ahead of the wagon, but still in sight of the family. As he slowly moved west on the rough road, he thought about what his ma had read earlier. Job, a good man, had all kinds of problems. The wealthy Israelite had lost thousands of camels, sheep, and donkeys. His family of ten had been killed by a cyclone. And, he had developed a terrible disease, much like the leprosy of the Bible. As David glanced ahead, he thought, why did God allow all of this?

"What good does it do to show love to a God like this — or is there a God?" he muttered. He remembered Lillie — who the preacher got, because he was holy. The poor Indians, and even worse, the slaves at the auction — were they all evil? He knew Lillie was not evil. He remembered one evening that they had almost had sex.

"No, David, I can't. I truly love you, but it's not right. God wouldn't approve," she had said.

David thought, what good did it get us? The fat preacher got her and I had to move away. He wondered about this God that he had been told about since he was four years old. His thoughts were interrupted when three deer darted out of the woods and ran across the road.

"Old mule, that venison would have tasted good tonight," David said out loud. As he looked back in the direction from where the deer came, he noticed why they were scared. Off to his right he saw an old house, sitting on stacks of rocks. Out to the east of the house was a vegetable garden of considerable size. Four members of the family were hoeing and working the garden. A middle-aged man was plowing with an old hand plow. The woman was hoeing while the two teenagers were pulling weeds. The man looked up and waved and David waved back. They looked to be in pretty bad shape, and he wondered how they made it.

As he glanced down the road, David thought, this is certainly no land of milk and honey. Nearing the noon hour, he came up on another wagon that was parked near the left side of the road. Needing to stretch his legs, he pulled on the mule's reins and stopped. Everyone appeared to be on the other side of the wagon. He got off the mule and started across the road to the wagon.

"Hey, fix me a plate of fried chicken," he yelled as he rounded the wagon, and then he stopped. A couple of men and a woman were lowering a body into a shallow grave that they had dug.

"Oh, I'm sorry; didn't know," he said, now embarrassed. He continued to stand there reverently until they had lowered the body to the bottom of the grave. "What happened?" he asked, lowering his voice to a whisper.

"Sister — came down with something, maybe 'monia. Been sick fer quite a spell; died last night."

David noticed tears in the man's eyes.

"You need any help?" he asked, looking at the other family members.

"Naw, we going to find us a place and settle down — thought 'bout along here," said the man.

"You know who owns this land?" asked David.

"Don't care who does. We'll move in wherever we likes," the man said in a defiant manner."

"Well, wish you lota luck," David said, and turned and walked back to the mule. As he walked, he thought, squatters. He remembered several squatters back in Tennessee. It was difficult to get them to move once they settled into a place.

David got back on his mule, looked back at the people, and then rode on toward Little Rock. Then he remembered that he had not eaten lunch. He turned the mule and started back east toward the wagon and his family. After a mile or so, he saw the wagon. His family had stopped to fix lunch. As he approached the wagon, he saw that Junior had started walking to meet him. As David drew closer, he dismounted and continued walking toward his little brother.

"We got more problems," Junior said, looking at David.

"What now?" asked David, his curiosity rising.

"Becky's pregnant."

"How do you know?" David asked, looking back toward the wagon.

"She was sick again this morning — throwed up. Ma just finally asked her if she ever had sex with Orville. She said only four times. Wow, I never saw Ma so mad! She has been ranting about Orville all morning. I feel sorry for Becky."

David knew it was probably true, since he had seen Becky riding Orville in the hay.

"Poor Becky," he said, looking ahead to the family members. By then, the two brothers had reached the wagon, with David leading the mule. Everyone was eating except Becky, who was in the wagon. David got a bowl and filled it with the soup that

Rachel and Sarah had prepared. There was little talking among the family members.

David poured a cup of coffee and then sat down near William. He had hardly put his cup down on the ground before William whispered, "Guess Junior told you Becky has shamed the whole family?"

"Yes, I heard, but there's nothing we can do now. I'm sure Becky is hurt more than anyone in the family. No use making it worse."

"Agree, but can you guess what Pa will say — he may go back and hang Orville from a tree, fifty feet high," replied his older brother.

"Might do it, but remember, Becky wasn't raped," said David. He thought, may have been other way 'round.

"You reckon Ma told her about sex?" questioned David. "You know, Pa never told us'uns about sex."

"Come on, David. We's all reared on the farm. We learns sex and birth from the livestock. She's seen the bull mount the cows — she's no child," said William.

"You probably right, but we still have to forgive her. Least that's what we's been taught by our parents," David said, glancing back toward his ma.

Later that evening, Becky finally left the wagon. Rachel talked to her for a while as they got out bedding.

It was a beautiful evening. A full moon and thousands of beautiful stars lit up the sky. Coyotes yelped in the distance. The sound of an occasional hoot owl added to the perfect evening. As David lay in his blanket, looking up at the Milky Way, he again thought of Lillie. Could she be looking out a window at the same wonderful evening? As he thought about the events of the day, he wished that it were Lillie who had been impregnated by him. She would be here — right in the same blanket with him. He drifted off to sleep thinking about his past love.

The next day, they spotted two more wagons moving in front of them. By evening, the Loflands had caught the other wagons at the small town of Palestine. With the area's only gristmill, the town was a popular place to meet and talk with friends.

The following morning, Sarah and the two girls took corn down to the mill. The brothers, except for Wilburn, went down to a small store where several men had gathered. The local men were discussing the current political situation in Little Rock.

"Who you'uns voting fer the governor?" asked a slightly built man, who was standing.

"Not Johnson. I'm going with the new feller, Rector; he's not mixed up with that crowd — Conway and his crooked group. They's stole enough money over there in Little Rock; we needs a change, and Rector sounds like the right man," prompted a thin man with a patch over one eye.

David waited until the speaker had quit talking.

"How'do," greeted another man. None of the other men greeted the newcomers.

"By the way, you'uns know how much farther on to Little Rock?" David asked, looking around at the men.

"Rite close to sixty mile if you'uns stay on same road," answered the man who had been complaining about the political situation. "But ya gonna have to ferry over the White River up 'round DeValls Bluff. The Bluff is 'bout forty or so."

Before William could respond, a third member of the group stood up, grasped his suspenders with both hands, and looked at the new arrivals.

"Ya'll not squatters, are ya?"

David had glanced back toward the mill to check on the womenfolk. Now he quickly turned back to face the speaker.

"No, we not; are you'uns?"

William turned to his younger brother, ready to calm him down. The former speaker, realizing that he had offended the Loflands, changed his tone.

"Well, jest askin'. We sees lot of 'em now'days. They thinks all the land is free."

David had now turned, along with Junior, and started back to their wagon. Seeing them leaving, William also followed his younger brothers back to the wagon. Wilburn had finished watering the oxen and was taking a drink.

"That didn't take long," the older brother said, lowering the dipper.

"The welcoming committee didn't 'xactly hug our necks. Not sure yet 'bout these Arkys," David said, looking back toward the store.

William had now got to the wagon.

"Said forty to a ferry crossing and 'bout sixty to Little Rock."

"Hmm, further than we thought. Bet pa's 'head of us now. He may git there week before we do," said William, patting the head of one of the oxen.

"They weren't too friendly, that right?" Wilburn asked William.

"Well, ole boy, he same as accused us of being squatters," replied William.

Wilburn — whom everyone said had his father's temper — quickly looked back to the store where the four men were sitting. Then, he rapidly started walking in that direction. William, with a disposition more like his mother, stepped in front of his older brother and grabbed him.

"Hold it, Wilburn; we don't need any more trouble."

The bigger Wilburn pushed William aside without a word and continued toward the store. He didn't notice that David was also following him. The big man with the suspenders, seeing Wilburn rapidly approaching, slowly stood up. Wilburn stepped up on the low porch where the men were sitting. The other man appeared to be ready, if he had to defend himself.

"You one of the squatters?" asked the big man as Wilburn took a couple of steps toward him, and then laughed.

When Wilburn's left foot hit the porch floor, his right arm was already coming around his muscular chest with a clenched fist. The man's effort to dodge was a second late. Wilburn's fist caught his face under his left eye and slightly left of his sharp nose. The startled man went backwards, landed on his back, and continued to slide down the porch floor and almost off the end of the porch.

The other three men had all stood up as Wilburn approached. David was prepared to take on the next challenger.

"Ferrell sometimes says too much," the tall, slender man reported. The man on his back, slightly dazed, was taking his time getting up. One of the men walked over to help their friend to his feet. The fallen man's nose was bleeding and his left eye was partially closed.

"I'll have the sheriff after you'uns," he said, looking up at Wilburn.

"Go rite ahead," replied David as the two Lofland brothers turned and started back to their wagon. William, witnessing the encounter, left to fetch the women.

"Couldn't tell you cut alota wood, big brother. I thought ole boy was going to slide all the way off the porch," said David, laughing.

"Might not have been the right thing to do though," said Junior, although he was also laughing. "That fourth feller looked about Becky's age. Might have run off a good prospect."

"Don't mention it to Ma, and the girls, or even Pa," said Wilburn. "We better go, in case they do try to contact the sheriff."

The women were surprised that they were leaving so soon.

"We's visiting with couple of nice ladies," said Sarah.

"Ma, their husbands weren't as friendly," said David, looking back toward the store.

In ten minutes, the Loflands were on the road again, headed toward Little Rock. Wilburn took the mule while William drove the oxen. Sarah, sitting in the wagon seat with William and David, asked how far it was to Little Rock.

"They said 'bout sixty mile — be another six days or so," replied William.

Chapter 10

Independence Day

BY LATE AFTERNOON, THE Loflands had reached the small town of Wheatley. Just west of the town was a sizable creek they had to cross. Wilburn, now ahead on the mule, carefully examined the low water crossing and concluded that they could get safely across. He proceeded across the creek on the mule and over a slight incline. As William directed the wagon down to the low water crossing, they heard horses behind them. William pulled up the oxen.

"They's three riders," said Junior, who was sitting on the back of the wagon. "One of them is the one that Wilburn flattened back there."

"What's this?" asked Sarah, looking quickly back to William. By then the riders had caught up to the wagon. A husky rider on a beautiful, black horse reached up and touched his hat.

"Ma'am, I'm the sheriff of Lonoke County. One of the men in Palestine has filed charges ag'in one of your men.

"Recognize the man," asked the sheriff, looking over at the man with the terrible black eye.

"Don't see him with these guys. He was a bigger feller."

"Mind if we check your wagon?" asked the sheriff.

"No, go rite ahead," replied William. The sheriff went around to the back of the big wagon and looked inside.

"Evening," he said to the girls and Junior. After looking around the area, he went back to the other two riders.

"Shor this is the family?" he asked, looking toward the man with the swollen eye.

"Well ask 'em if they had another feller with 'em," replied the man, somewhat irritated at the sheriff.

"We had a feller that caught a ride for awhile. He got off 'bout five mile back. Big, husky guy," replied David, looking straight at the officer.

"Sounds like 'round Goodwin," the sheriff said, immediately wheeling his horse about.

The three men quickly rode off in the other direction. Meanwhile, in the opposite direction, Wilburn, on the mule, had watched the activity from behind a big cedar tree. He surmised that the riders might have been the law.

As William drove the oxen on across the creek, Sarah demanded to know what had happened earlier. Over the next ten minutes, William explained what had happened at Palestine, including the men's threat to contact the sheriff. Sarah did not take the explanation very well, although she was glad that Wilburn had not been arrested.

"Wilburn should have minded his own business. We may hear more of this later on," she said with a glare.

Sarah took it better than David thought she would. About two miles down the road, Wilburn moved out of the woods, leading the mule.

"Did they leave?" he asked, looking over at David. David explained to his brother what he had told the Lonoke sheriff.

"Man, you think fast; you probably kept me out of jail," replied Wilburn. Glancing back at Sarah, he saw the stern look she gave him. "Sorry, Ma. I lost my temper, I guess."

"I guess you did! You better stay up front with the mule at

least for a while, in case that sheriff figures out what happened."

"Wilburn, if the sheriff comes back, I will blow the old coon-hunting horn, okay," said David.

"Good idea. See ya'll," Wilburn said, and then rode back west in front of the wagon.

In a little more an hour, the family had reached the White River. Wilburn, waiting there, had already made arrangements to ferry the family over to the west side of the river. William carefully eased the oxen onto the waiting ferry. Once they were on board, a man on the east side of the river blew a loud horn.

On the west side of the river, a man with a winch began to shorten the rope attached to the barge, causing the ferry barge to move toward the far bank. When it was almost in the middle of the river, they heard a splash near the back of the wagon — and then a scream.

"Ma, Becky jumped into the river!" cried Rachel, who had seen her sister as she hit the water.

David, sitting on the right side of the wagon seat, quickly turned back to look to the rear of the wagon. Realizing what had happened, he quickly jerked off his boots and dived into the water.

Not realizing there was a problem, the winch attendant on the far shore kept pulling the barge toward the west shore. Sarah screamed at the same time there was a second splash. William had also removed his boots, and he quickly joined David in the river.

As the family now anxiously watched from the barge, David came up to get fresh air — then down he went again, frantically searching for his sister. Then he came up again, and the terrified family saw Becky's head. David was swimming on his right side, stroking mainly with his right arm. Becky was under his left arm.

William, swimming vigorously, finally got to David and Becky, and he also grabbed hold of his sister. Within a couple of minutes, David and William reached water shallow enough that they could stand up. Becky had now regained consciousness, and the two brothers walked her over to the west shore of the river.

By then, the rest of the family had hurried off the ferry barge and had run down to the area where the boys were bringing Becky out of the water. Sarah, crying, hurried out into the shallow water, grabbed her daughter, and tightly hugged her. Rachel, behind Sarah, was also crying and waiting her turn to hug her twin sister.

After getting Becky out of the water, the boys helped her sit down. She was still frantically coughing, trying to expel water from her lungs. William and Junior began to gather wood for a fire and Sarah fetched a blanket for her shivering daughter. The whole family was soon gathered around the fire.

"I wanted to die. I shamed the whole family, and Pa don't even know yet," said Becky, looking at Sarah.

"Becky, I'm speaking for your whole family. We are all ashamed for failing to support you in a time of need. You needed our support and we failed. We are sorry," said Wilburn with a shaky voice. There was not a dry eye around the fire after he finished speaking. "And one more thing; David was a real hero to dive in so quickly to save Becky."

"Thanks, David," Becky softly said.

He reached over and gently hugged his sister. After everyone had consoled and hugged Becky, they extinguished the fire and everyone went back to the wagon. William asked all to bow as he offered a prayer of thanks to God for Becky's rescue.

With the loss of two hours, the Loflands boarded the wagon and again set out for Little Rock. David noticed that each member of the family seemed to realize how close tragedy had come to them that day. As the wagon rolled along, he wondered who saved Becky — was it him, or was it God? He wondered, if Becky had drowned, should they have blamed God? He didn't know, but he wondered how much the creator observed his creation.

He thought back to earlier in the day when the sheriff arrived to arrest Wilburn. Then he had left in the opposite direction, riding hard, hoping to catch Wilburn. Thank God, someone had said. Would God have approved of the black lie that he told — that Wilburn was a stranger that had hitched a ride with them? If we had told the truth, Wilburn would be in jail, David thought; I disregarded the morality of lying and saved big brother from a jail sentence. It wasn't God who had prevented William's arrest. Did God even care?

David continued to think about this as the wagon moved west. He thought, prayer maybe is all right, but sometimes we can't wait and see if God cares. However, David thought he would not mention his feelings to the other family members. He wondered, is it even necessary to take time to pray? Then he thought of his pa. How was he doing? What about Lillie? Would she attempt something like Becky? No, she was too good a Christian to consider that. The greedy parson had used his so-called faith to convince Lillie to marry him. If there was a hell, he hoped the fat preacher would wind up there.

"Man, look at that spread," David said with awe, as he looked over to the north side of the road. There was a magnificent, plantation home in the distance. As they drew closer, the Loflands could see the beautiful fields on each side of the home. Several large trees lined the drive leading up to the house. Colorful azaleas bloomed near the home. Out in the field nearby, fifty or sixty Negro slaves chopped cotton or thinned out the plants that crowded each other. Some of the darkies were singing. Several stopped working and waved at the passing wagon.

Sarah and the girls waved back at the slaves. As the wagon got even with the mansion, David noticed that all of his family members were admiring the home. The huge columns up to the second floor were impressive. Out on the veranda, a white-coated, black servant served a man and woman food and drink. A big dog lay by the man on the porch.

"The Lord has really blessed that couple," observed Sarah, as the Loflands slowly passed the huge home. By then, the wagon had passed enough of the mansion for the passengers to be able to see out beyond the big house. In the distance, they could see ten or twelve slave cabins. Several black children played close by, cared for by an old black woman.

"Reckon those darkies are being blessed?" asked David. No one answered his question.

"William, look for a place to stop so we can eat and maybe camp for the night," said Sarah.

"Okay, Ma," replied William, glancing back toward the plantation. They had probably traveled a half-mile when David turned back to his ma.

"They's a small clearing up ahead with a shelter over some poles — maybe a bush arbor."

"That would be fine," Sarah responded.

William directed the oxen into the clearing. Everyone was eager to get out and stretch their legs. Walking over to the shelter, Rachel noticed some roughly constructed benches.

"Ma, looks like the church arbor back home. Someone must have a church meeting here," she said as she walked around the crude structure.

"Believe it's a meetin' place," said Wilburn, who had just ridden up on the mule.

"You think it's safe to join us ag'in?" William asked his older brother.

"I think so. If they were following us, they would have caught us back there at the ferry crossing," replied Wilburn. "Besides, I need to rest my fanny and let you or David ride the mule a while."

The womenfolk had begun to remove food from the wagon.

"David, will you build a fire," Sarah asked.

"You bet, Ma," answered David, looking around the arbor. "Help me find some wood, Junior."

While the women prepared supper, William fed some of the corn to the oxen.

"What we having, Ma? I could eat a rat rite now," he exclaimed, looking over at the pots and pans.

"We having a big kettle of stew probably eat on it for days, replied Rachael as David and Wilburn took the yoke off the oxen.

"You guys did a good job today," Wilburn said, slapping one of the oxen on the rump.

While the women prepared the meal, David noticed that Becky was humming as she worked. He was glad that she no longer seemed to be distressed.

"Stew's ready; come get a bowl," Sarah soon called out to the men. As the family lined up to get their supper, they heard voices in the distance.

"Sounds like singing," said Becky, looking out to the road. As the sound grew closer, they could tell that it was several people singing. Then a wagon came into sight. A middle-aged white man drove the wagon, carrying at least twenty black people. When he reached the arbor clearing, the driver turned the oxen into it. The blacks could now see the Lofland wagon; the singing slowed and then stopped.

David realized that this was the Negro church's bush arbor. The driver stopped the oxen and stepped down from the wagon. None of the black people moved. Since William was the closest to the newcomers, the white man walked over to him.

"Howdy. Burns, overseer at Cedar Vale plantation back up the road. This arbor is part of our property. It is also the church meeting place for our niggers. We 'lowed them to have a revival this week, as long as they met their quota. They more than met it, so we kept our word. You'uns don't have to go — can stay here or join in, but I wanted you to know."

Well, thanks. Is it okay to camp here for the night?" asked William, who was studying the overseer.

"Sure. Make ya self at home," said Burns, looking back at the wagon and waving.

Again, much chatter as the black people clamored down and moved toward their meeting place. A couple of the black women had tambourines and a couple had homemade drums. One older man had an old mandolin.

The Loflands moved back to their fire, filled their bowls with stew, and settled down to watch. The overseer climbed back into the wagon to both watch and stand guard. The black man with the mandolin moved to one end of the arbor, preparing to lead the group. The others, all adults, sat down on the old benches.

"Come, Thou Fount," said the leader.

With good, firm voices, and great enthusiasm, the group sang, "Come, Thou Fount of every blessing." After the third verse, the Loflands broke out in heavy applause.

"Praise the Lord," cried out Sarah.

The leader followed with, "Holy, Holy, Holy." This song was even better, as the mandolin, the drums, and the tambourines combined for an impressive beat.

"And now, 'Redeemed,'" shouted the leader.

David was sure that the plantation owners back up the road could hear the song. He had to admit that the singing was beautiful. As the song ended, Sarah walked over to the black leader with the mandolin.

"We have made a big pot of stew. Would ya'll come and share it with us?"

The surprised black leader looked over to the overseer, who nodded his approval.

"We's been 'vited to eat stew wiv da white folk," the black leader announced, looking back at the Negroes. "Din I's preaching after we eats."

The group quickly filed over to the Loflands' wagon, where Rachel handed out containers of all kinds to hold the stew. The Loflands were friendly to the slaves, and the slaves were quite talkative. After the meal was over, the leader asked the Loflands if they would like to come over and worship with them. The family members politely followed the blacks over to the arbor and took the back seats. The leader, who was also the pastor, looked at the combined group and prepared to speak.

"We's gathered here to worship and praise da Lord."

"Amen," someone said.

"The Lord tells us in da Word dat he is da Sheeperd. We knows what sheeperds do. They's don't chop cotton or pick it neither."

"Amen."

"Sheeperds fights off wolves and bobcats like one dat almost kilt Mammy Colin," said, the preacher, raising his voice. "They's not scared — even of black bears."

"Glory."

"Yes, our Sheeperd walks with us'uns every day, even in de night."

"Amen."

"He give his life fo' his sheeps — ya hear me — fo' his sheeps."

"Amen."

"Don't reckon anyone here ever did dat, or ya wouldn't be here."

"Amen."

"The sheeperd keeps his'n sheeps in de corral. He guards 'em good."

"Halaluya."

"If"n a robber opens dat corral gate, dat sheeperd's there quicker 'n lightnin'."

"Amen. Amen."

"If he catches de robber — twenty licks with de overseer's whip."

David glanced over at the overseer, who was smiling.

"Now, some time, sheeps git out'a corral and runs away, kin' like a runaway slave. Know wat? Dat sheeperd gits on his mule and looks all over de place fer 'em. He leaves ones in de corral, hopes they don't run off, and goes to fetch the runaway."

"Amen."

"He gist back to da corral. They happy and has stew good as we'ed had 'while go. What a sheeperd we'uns has. Say Amen; again, Amen. Okay, let's finish wiv 'When Roll is Called Up Yonder.'"

After the fourth verse, the preacher prayed and the slaves began to move back to their wagon. The overseer counted the slaves and then flipped the reins of the mules. The slaves waved and some called out good-byes to the Loflands. As the slave wagon left, Sarah started back to the fire with the girls to wash all of the dishes that the large group had used.

"Was a nice service — a little different, but they could sing. Good to know that slaves are also believers."

"Can't figure why, Lord don't seem to help them much. He must favor white folks," said David.

"David, I'm worried about you lately. You sound like one of them atheists. Have you lost your faith?"

"No, don't think so. I am mixed up about some things."

"Well I hope not," said Sarah.

The Loflands made it to Little Rock, the capital of Arkansas, in two weeks. The river city was not quite as big as Memphis; however, on occasions, it served as a river port. The Arkansas River, at certain times of the year, was navigable from the Mississippi River to Pine Bluff and on up to the capital. However, during times of drought or little rainfall, the river was not deep enough for the larger steamboats.

The Loflands arrived at the Arkansas River, just east of Little Rock, on June 1, 1861. It was now warm, with hardly any wind blowing. With little rain for the last two months, the Loflands had made good progress. It was necessary to ferry across the Arkansas River. Once again, Wilburn made the arrangements with the ferry service. Fortunately, the cost was only a dollar.

After a smooth crossing, Wilburn again asked for directions for the route west of Little Rock. A man, who had identified himself as a deputy sheriff, gave Wilburn directions.

"First, you got to go to Ola. Can't go directly west 'cause you'ed run into the Ouachita Mountains and alot of forest — no roads there anyway. Outside town, they's a road going northwest to Perryville. Once there, ask, 'cause they's two roads you could take there going west. Again, take the road outside and stay on it till you get outside Little Rock. They's a new cotton gin there where you will turn off for Perryville and Ola — don't forget that."

"That was very plain," William said, grinning.

The Loflands made one stop at a dry goods store. Sarah bought some cloth that she could use for dresses for the girls.

While in the store, they overheard the storeowner talking to a customer.

"Yeah, we heered it today. Earlier in April they's a fight back east between Northerns and Southerds. The Southerds fired cannon on a Federal fort — Fort Sumter, round Charleston, South Carolina. Fight went on whole day before the Federals surrendered. They done let the Federals go back home. Reckon we won the first battle."

"How many killed?" David asked.

"None killed atall," the storeowner replied. "Course, we surely in war now with the Northerns."

As David walked back to the wagon, he wondered how a war would affect their lives. He knew that trouble had been brewing, but he never thought that the country would go to war.

"Bad news, men," David said when he reached the wagon. "War started back in Carolini. We won first battle — hope it's the last one."

"That could be bad, 'specially since there are three of us that are fightin' age," Wilburn said.

"Bet Pa knows about it already," Junior said, looking looked back at Wilburn.

"Well — we'll just wait and see what happens," Wilburn added, switching the oxen.

Leaving the outskirts of Little Rock, the family noticed that the road was more crooked and steeper. They were definitely moving into more hilly terrain. The oxen, already with the heavy load, worked much harder now. Wilburn, driving the oxen, suggested that everyone but Sarah get off the wagon and walk.

Sarah continued to drive the oxen. On the mule about half-mile ahead of the group, David noticed that there were no homes in this hilly, forested area. As he rode on, he wondered about his pa. Could he already be at Bluffton waiting for the family? Probably not; if he had reached Bluffton, the first thing he would do was start out on horseback to meet them. He would have to watch for his pa.

As he thought about a new home in Arkansas, David noticed two men approaching on horseback from the west. Within minutes, the men were close enough that David could see a trailing lone man, walking behind the mounted riders. The man, a Negro, had manacle chains on his hands, attached to leg irons. The chains between the leg irons were short, and in order to keep up with his captor's horses, the man had to take short, quick steps. The Negro was shirtless and barefooted. The bottoms of his feet were bloody from scraping the rocky road.

The riders stopped when they got to David and the mule.

"Howdy; going to Perryville?" asked a slightly cross-eyed man. David noticed a badge on his shirt.

"Yeah. We's really headed for Bluffton; you been there?" asked David.

"Shor — next county. We's taking the nigger to Little Rock; done gone and killed his owner. A no-good preacher there was raping the nigger's sister, who's only nine years old. And 'cording to the nigger, he done it before."

David glanced over at the captive, who was staring at his bloody feet.

"What'll they do to him?" asked David.

"Oh, they'll hang him 'fore the weekend. Shame they didn't get the preacher man — should've hung him. Course, you know how it goes; his flock defended him. None of them believed he was a rapist. I believe the girl was telling the truth though. You may hear more when you git amongst 'em in Perryville."

David glanced back down the road where the wagon was in

sight, and then looked back at the man with the badge.

"That's my family coming."

"Well, take care," the man said as the threesome moved on, with the Negro once again taking short, quick steps to keep up with his captors.

David rode on, thinking about the conversation. A preacher, probably a fat preacher, had raped a girl of nine, probably on a regular basis, and the church folks, high and mighty, believed the preacher. No doubt, such vermin could easily fool folks. He thought, men of God? Hypocrites that use people to get what they want. Looks like God would punish them, instead of people like the poor nigger who would leave a young sister behind — probably to be raped many more times.

The Loflands reached Perryville three days later. It was July 4, and the town had prepared a big celebration for the occasion. A platform had been erected in the town square. Not far away were several tables with all kinds of food, from beef to wild turkey, to strawberry shortcake. Everyone was invited to participate.

After parking the oxen and wagon under a big walnut tree, William helped the women down from the wagon. The other men, already off the wagon, were stretching and limbering up from the long day's ride. Several people spoke to the new arrivals as they moved on through the town square.

By then a man had climbed the platform steps and was looking out over the crowd. He held a bullhorn in his hand.

"Friends and neighbors, enjoy the delicious food," he addressed the small crowd. "Also, cold cider and whiskey over to my right. Enjoy. Our mayor will speak in thirty or forty minutes."

The meal was the best that the Loflands had eaten since their going away church dinner in Hickory Flats. William met a young lady about his age and sat down to eat with her. David noticed that Rachael was drawing some serious attention from some of the locals. Becky, now showing signs of her pregnancy, stayed near her mother. Junior had wandered over to an area where some young teenagers were playing mumblety–peg with pocketknives. Wilburn, as usual, was inquiring about the best route to Bluffton.

A short, heavy man soon climbed the platform steps and then paused, as if out of breath. He was well dressed, with a shiny, gold-colored vest covered by a light brown jacket. He'd already removed a well-shaped hat that he carried in his right hand. David noticed the sun reflecting off the man's bald head.

Almost everyone had finished their meal and was now looking at the town's mayor. Sensing that the crowd was ready, the man, with some difficulty, moved to the railing at the front of the platform. He chose not to use the bullhorn.

"Friends and guests of Perry County, welcome to our annual Independence Day celebration. If you haven't finished eating, go right ahead; won't bother me. I ate so much, I could hardly climb the steps."

A few people laughed. The mayor wiped his mouth with a handkerchief and looked over the crowd below.

"About eighty years ago, our founding fathers gathered to read what Thomas Jefferson wrote a little earlier, our Declaration of Independence. We didn't get our independence by reading that document — we had to go out on the battlefield and win our independence. Cost many lives and fortunes before we could be our own country with our own government. Many of us lost relatives and even families in that war for independence. King George III increased our taxes and made all kinds of demands on us Americans."

The mayor reached for his handkerchief and blew his nose.

A couple of the younger children laughed at the strange noise.

"What heroes we cherish — Washington, Jefferson, Madison and Monroe," he continued. "They built this country for us."

The crowd applauded for the first time.

"But, friends, do you remember that all four of those presidents owned slaves? Washington, said to be the father of our country, may have been the country's biggest slaveholder. But after them, they's more presidents that owned slaves. Men like Jackson, Taylor, Tyler, and Polk. As you know, the abolitionists up north are clamoring for the elimination of slavery. We done gone and elected the Lincoln feller, who may try to free the slaves — if he beats us in war. Can you imagine what would happen if three or four million slaves in the South were freed? They would try to slaughter everyone, including women and children. Just look at what happened in our own fair city last week. A beloved pastor of one of our churches left behind a wonderful wife and daughter after his male slave rose up to kill him for no reason — a man that had fed and cared for the Negro and his own sister. And furthermore, the killer and his sister made up a lie straight from hell itself about Pastor Hainy. This man of God loved the two Negroes."

There was more applause from the crowd. You right about the preacher loving one of the Negroes, David thought — but it was only the female. As the mayor went on, David wondered, how big a tombstone would the people put up for the hypocrite's grave in the cemetery? After a drink of water, the speaker continued.

"The country is more divided than it's ever been. Most Northerners are for war against us here in the South. They would tear up the Constitution that permits slavery and stick it down our throats."

"No," cried out several people in the crowd.

"We didn't select the right man for the presidency in 1860. We needed a man with Southern roots, a man who understands our beloved, Southern culture. Hopefully, this man can be restrained before this country faces even more serious war."

Again, there was more applause.

"Let's pray to the Almighty that this war will end soon. Thank you and enjoy your day."

As the crowd began to move slowly away from the town square, the Loflands walked back to their wagon.

"Good speech," said Wilburn. "Ole boy knows what he's talking about all right."

"No, wasn't bad at all," agreed William.

As David trailed his older brothers, he thought, that slave-owning preacher was more highly thought of than the founding fathers.

"What'd you think, David?" asked Junior.

"It was all right, but I git the idea that both sides, the North and the South, are sure that God is on their side. Bet God's confused."

Rachel arrived at the wagon last, after talking with the young man from Perryville. David was glad that the other twin was getting some attention from the opposite sex.

Chapter 11

Bluffton

IN TWO DAYS, THE family had arrived at Nimrod. Later, using an old road that followed the Fourche River, the Loflands made it to Plainview by nightfall of the third day. That evening Becky and Rachel cooked several large catfish that the men had caught in the river. Everyone bragged on the twin cooks and their great meal.

By then, the young Lofland men were very worried about their pa. He should have arrived in Bluffton much earlier and come to meet them. While they worried about their pa, the men assured the women that they were sure that everything was all right.

The postal official at Plainview had told Wilburn that Bluffton was eighteen miles west. He said that they might make it in a day if they left early enough the next morning. No one needed any urging to get up early, and by 6:00 a.m. the family was on the road to Bluffton. William was up ahead of the wagon on the mule. With relatively flat land to travel now, all the family members except for Wilburn and David rode on the wagon.

Except for a small problem with the ox yoke, everything went well. The family stopped and ate lunch at the small town of Briggsville. Sarah announced that they had eaten all of the salted pork and ham. However, bacon and beans satisfied the appetite of everyone, and with little time lost, they were moving again toward Bluffton.

"I'm worried about Pa," Wilburn said as he checked the ox yoke again. "He should have been here by now."

"The storeowner at Briggsville knew Seth, but he had heard nothing of Pa," exclaimed Wilburn, anxiously looking down the road toward Bluffton.

"I've been worried ever since we left," stated Sarah. "But we have got to trust God; we are in his care." No one saw David slightly shake his head, as if he couldn't believe what his ma had said.

They had traveled about five miles west of Briggsville when William, now on the scout mule, met another man in a field wagon. He waved at William just before they met. The older man, a small, soft-spoken man with gray hair, asked if William had seen a wagon anywhere behind as he traveled west.

"Got family coming. John Lofland's family from Tennessee."

"You're not Uncle Seth?" William asked, smiling.

"Sure am; and which boy are you? Wilburn?"

"No, I'm William. Second oldest."

"Thank the Lord, and John is with you?" questioned the relieved uncle.

"No, Uncle Seth. We haven't seen pa since Memphis. We thought he'd already be here."

"I've come out the last five days looking for ya'll," Seth said, frowning. "Now I'm really worried about my younger brother. Is the wagon far back?"

"I reckon 'bout mile or so," replied William. "Uncle Seth, let's wait here for the rest of the family and then go on to your house. But I gotta tell you, ma's really afraid that something happened to pa."

The wagon came into sight in a few minutes. Family members, looking ahead, could see William up ahead on his mule along with a second man.

"Is it John?" asked a worried Sarah.

"Don't think so, Ma," responded Wilburn. "Not big enough. Could be Uncle Seth, though."

When Wilburn stopped the wagon near the two men, everyone recognized the uncle. They all quickly jumped down to greet Seth.

"It's so good to see you again," Seth said as Sarah hugged him. "I've missed you so."

"We've missed you too," Sarah said to her older brother-in-law. "You haven't seen John?"

"No, Sarah. We have had no word. I hoped he was with ya'll, but don't worry; he'll show up."

David noticed the tears in both their eyes. It was obvious to Seth that the girls were just as worried about John as their ma.

After traveling about three miles down the road, they arrived at Seth's home. Seth's wife, Aunt Allie, had heard the wagons coming and was already out on the porch waiting for them.

When the Loflands had exchanged greetings with Allie, they had a chance to look around at the small, respectable home. Fireplaces stood at each end of the three-bedroom, two-level home. A porch extended from the roof out over a rough balcony, which ran the length of the house and served as a porch cover. A door on the second level led out to the balcony. Below the balcony was the main door, with a window on each side of it. Surrounded by a cedar rail fence, the well-constructed home was made of squared logs. In between the logs was a white chinking.

While no news of John dampened spirits that evening, everyone enjoyed talking about times back in Tennessee, when

Seth and Allie had lived there. Aunt Allie, as all knew, was an excellent cook. Everyone really enjoyed the pecan pie that she had made. Seth, eight years senior to John, had three cows, a couple of goats, pigs, and chickens. Even with his age, he and Allie had done a good job providing for themselves. Allie had given birth to two children, a boy and a girl. Both had died of yellow fever shortly after moving to Arkansas.

After the wonderful dinner and while the women were doing dishes, Wilburn asked Seth if they could go out and sit on the front porch.

"Fine; let me get my pipe tobacco," Seth said. After the men were seated on the porch, he spoke up. "Tired hearing ya'll call me uncle — Seth is fine with me. Everybody got that?"

"Okay, Seth," Wilburn said. "Tomorrow, take us down to the property that pa wants to buy. We can even pick out a home site. We may mark some trees to cut — trees we can use in building. We'll go ahead and make some plans, 'cause day after tomorrow I'm headed for Little Rock to see if Pa ever arrived there. May be gone a month or so, but William, David, and Junior can git started on the home. They's all good with saw and hammer. You could boss them along and give advice, 'cause you already built a nice home here."

"Will, you lot like pa — want to do things by yourself. One of us'uns needs to go with you — could be dangerous," argued William, looking at his older brother.

"Appreciate it, Bill, but building a home before winter is high priority. It will take all three of you, Seth, and the girls. No, I will take the mule and I can move much faster."

"Well, don't knock anyone off any porches while you're gone," said David.

All laughed, although Seth did not know what they were laughing about.

The next day, all the men left on the wagon to look at land that Seth had recommended to John. The first part of the journey was to go south down the road that passed Seth's home. When they had reached the forty acres, Seth directed the oxen down in a pasture dotted with several large, pecan trees. In the middle of the large field was a slight hill, with more large trees scattered about.

"That's it Wilburn — on top of the rise. That site is elevated, in case the river floods the field," stated William.

"I agree," said David. "Also plenty of room for a barn, smokehouse, and other outbuildings — what do you think, Junior?"

"It's good — that's the place, and not to many trees to cut there. But back a mile or so, they's lots trees for building."

"Why I brought you here first — great home site and those trees back to the west are near the Fourche River. It's bottomland at the best," exclaimed Seth. "Let's go mark the trees that we will remove and check for any bogs or wet places."

By lunchtime, the four men had marked twenty-four trees to be cut on the incline. They could also use most of the trees as construction material for the house. They marked another thirty-five trees to clear for farmland. They could also use these trees in the construction of the home. They marked other trees to create a drive off the road.

"Ma will be crazy about it, and there is even a spring just over the hill where we can put in a well. We will have a lot of rocks to pick up and move to the river, but Arkansas seems to have rocks everywhere," Wilburn said, gazing over the Fourche bottomlands.

Later, as they sat down for the noon meal, the men described the home site to the womenfolk. They were all excited as well.

"The Lord has already blessed us," said Sarah, smiling.

There were several "amens" from the group. As David put his fork into a big piece of ham hock, he thought, lets wait till we find pa before we get carried away.

Chapter 12

Return to Pine Bluff

BY 6:00 A.M., WILBURN was on the mule with a big sack of food provisions. He had his musket, hunting knife, shell and gunpowder, two blankets, and extra clothing. After a hug from Sarah, he was ready for the trip.

"Will, ya'll start on the trees today and have the place ready by the time me and Pa git back. And listen to Seth for his advice," he said while looking at Wilburn.

"Hey, big brother, find yourself a bride over at Little Rock," shouted David. "We'll let ya'll live in the new outhouse."

The boys laughed. Wilburn left on the mule, going east toward Briggsville and Little Rock. If the dark clouds didn't bring rain, he would ride until nightfall. By stopping only at nightfall to eat and sleep, Wilburn was able to reach the capital city in five days. After arriving in the capital, he didn't know who was more tired, the old gray mule or himself.

Following the same route that the family at taken earlier, in reverse, Wilburn soon came to the dry goods store that he had passed almost three weeks before. With several customers in the store, Wilburn had to wait a while to talk to the storeowner. After the man in front of him had completed his business, Wilburn stepped forward to the counter.

"What can I do for you?" asked the proprietor.

"Sur, can you give me directions to the Little Rock river port? Just there three weeks ago, but wanna make sure I'm on the rite road,"

"Stay on the road out front, River Road. Ya can't miss it — 'bout three mile or so," replied the storeowner as he turned to help another customer.

In less than an hour, Wilburn had reached the river port. Now he remembered where the port authority office was located. After reaching the office, he noticed a big sign on the door — Little Rock Port Authority. He opened the door and went inside. Two men were in the small office. One of the men sat behind a desk. The other was sitting in front of the desk, with his feet up on it. The men were laughing about something.

"Howdy. Can I help you?" the man at the desk finally said, looking up. The second man kept his eye on the visitor but didn't move.

"Sur, I'm Wilburn Lofland. My pa boarded a steamboat back in April at Memphis, with oxen and wagon and our family's furniture. He had a ticket to come to Little Rock where he planned on gitting off the ship and coming on to Bluffton — that's west of Ola."

The official behind the desk nodded as if to show he knew where Bluffton was.

"Pa never showed up, so I thought I'd see if he ever arrived at Little Rock," explained Wilburn, looking at the man behind the desk.

"First, what was his name?"

"John Lofland, sur."

"Okay. What date did he board the ship at Memphis?" asked the man.

"It was a Saturday, April 19," Wilburn replied, glancing back toward the second man.

"Okay. Let me check," said the official as he went over to a table behind the desk. On the table were two wooden boxes, both filled with papers. He selected the box that was marked "Received."

"And you said it was April 19; is that right?" the man said.

"Yes, sur," replied Wilburn, glancing around the office.

After going through about half of the papers in the box, the official suddenly stopped. He turned to look back at Wilburn.

"Mister, the Arkansas River was way down in April. The steamers could not move up river to Little Rock from April 18 through April 30. The first ship in here after that was May 3. I show no one coming into the Rock from May 3 till yesterday with the name Lofland." The man glanced up to the disappointed Wilburn. "But," the official continued, "ships did make it to the Bluff during that time."

"Whar's the Bluff?"

"Pine Bluff — seventy mile down river. However, this is not unusual — happens two, three times a year."

"Any idea you could give me 'bout what I should do?" asked Wilburn, who was much more worried now.

"Well, best thing would be to go down to the Bluff and see what they know. We really don't know if he ever got to Pine Bluff," the official related, looking back over to his friend. "One of these days, we'll have telegraph to Pine Bluff, but it is not here yet.

"You say Pine Bluff 'bout seventy miles?"

"Yeah. Take care," replied the official in a dismissive manner.

Wilburn left the office and walked back to where he had tied the mule.

"Sorry mule, but we got a trip even longer now," muttered Wilburn as he rubbed the mule's shoulder.

Without any further delay, Wilburn mounted the mule and

started south in the direction of Pine Bluff. He entered the outskirts of Pine Bluff four and a half days later, almost as tired as the mule. After getting directions, he rode further south to the Pine Bluff Port Office. Fortunately, no large ships were there and, consequently, very few people were near the dock area.

Wilburn noticed that the docking offices in Pine Bluff were small and less official looking than those in Little Rock. Three men were in a tiny office, talking about a recent fishing trip that they had taken. A short, stocky man was talking about a rendezvous with an alligator when Wilburn walked in through the open door.

"Who is in charge here?" asked the worried Wilburn, looking around at all three men.

"He is," said two of the men, pointing at each other as if neither wanted to help the newcomer.

"What can I do for you?" asked the stocky official who had finished laughing about the joke.

"On April 19, my pa, John Lofland, boarded a steamer in Memphis with oxen and a wagon filled with furniture. Never made it to Little Rock, so's I wonder if he ever got here."

A young black man had entered the office as Wilburn described the situation.

"If it was April 19 through April 28, no ships went up river due to low water and sand bars," interrupted the stocky port official before Wilburn had finished speaking. "If your pa came in during that time, he was told that he could be reimbursed three dollars and get off the boat and go north on his own, or that if he hung around Pine Bluff for a week or so — and the river came up, he could go on to Little Rock on the first ship. Your pa had to choose one of those options."

Wilburn, with a frown on his face, looked out the window at the river.

"Sur," said the young black, "yo pa a big man wive dark hair and a scar on his'en face?"

"Yes,"Wilburn quickly responded, hoping to get information on John.

"I's 'member him, 'cause he was a good driver of de oxen. Win he brought 'em on de ship, stayed with 'em most of de time. I seed him takes his wagon of'ten de ship."

One of the port officials looked up at Wilburn.

"If'en I's you, I'd go to the sheriff's office — just down the street. They may know som'in," the man suggested.

"I believe I passed the sheriff's office back there. I think I will go ask 'em if they know anything," Wilburn answered, looking down at the floor.

"Wish ya good luck," said the stocky port official. "Hope you find your pa."

"Thanks," said Wilburn. "And thanks to you," he said to the young black man who was still looking at him.

The sheriff was not in, but a young deputy sheriff was in the office reviewing wanted posters. He looked up when Wilburn entered.

"Sit down. What can I do for you?" the man said as he stacked the papers to one side of a desk that was against the wall.

Wilburn related the entire story to the young deputy.

"What was the date your pa arrived in Pine Bluff?" asked the deputy with an inquisitive look.

"April 19, a Saturday," answered Wilburn.

Looking as if he might know something, the deputy opened the desk drawer and checked other papers.

"Yow — April 20. How big was your pa?" the deputy asked.

"Little over six foot, two hundred pounds, big, muscular build. Well, I'm his oldest son — built lot like me," related Wilburn.

The deputy produced a piece of paper.

"We found a man 'bout three mile out — you probably passed the clearing — been murdered. Throat cut. We asked around and a man 'bout his size had been seen the day before driving oxen and wagon — with furniture — headed north toward Little Rock."

As he glanced back to Wilburn, the man noticed tears in his eyes. He was visibly shaken by the report.

"I'm sure sorry, but — wait. There was no papers at all on the deceased, but he did have a belt with an unusual belt buckle."

The man stood up, opened the storage room door, and went inside. He soon came out of the room with a belt in his hand. The deputy's glance at Wilburn told him that he recognized the belt buckle.

"A Cherokee made that buckle for Pa," said Wilburn in a broken voice. "It's his."

"I'm sorry," the deputy repeated.

With the belt in his hand, Wilburn thanked the sheriff and left the sheriff's office. As he rode back through town, he came to a dry goods store on the outskirts of Pine Bluff. Needing chewing tobacco, Wilburn went into the store. As he moved through it, he noticed a door leading into a large room. Going over to the door, he saw a variety of goods stacked around the walls. Several people were looking over the sale merchandise. As Wilburn started to move past the door leading into the sale display room, something caught his eye. He immediately stepped back into the doorway and looked across the room. Then he entered the room and walked over to the wall.

He thought he recognized it! It was William's and his bedroom dresser. He slowly pulled out the top drawer of the dresser. There, on the bottom of the drawer, scratched in the wood clearly, were the letters W.L. — his initials. Wilburn remembered the whipping that his pa had given him for scratching his initials in the wood when he was only ten years old.

He quickly turned and walked back into the main part of the store and over to the counter, where a heavy man was helping a farmer. When the farmer left, Wilburn stepped up to the counter.

"You know where you got that oak dresser in there?" Wilburn noticed that the store manager was definitely uneasy as he looked back at Wilburn.

"W- w- well. Let's see. Someone — don't recall who — brought that in couple weeks ago. I finally bought it. You interested in it?"

The man seemed to recover quickly. Wilburn suddenly grabbed the man's shirt collar, squeezed it tightly around his neck, and then pulled him halfway over the counter close to his own face. "My friend, you had better have the name of that person who sold you that dresser within two hours or I will tear this store down. Do you understand?"

Everyone in the store was now looking at the two men, most expecting to see the muscular Wilburn lift the store manager completely over the counter.

"Okay, okay. I'll try," muttered the man, his eyes still bulging from the near strangulation.

"I'll be back in two hours," Wilburn said as he moved away, still looking at the man.

None of the other customers had moved as they watched the confrontation. As Wilburn walked out of the store, the storeowner straightened his collar.

"Anybody know that hick?" he asked.

No one replied. The man quickly walked back into the large sale room and looked around.

"Buhl, come 'er."

A tall, thin man, about thirty years old, started toward the storeowner. Above the heavy stubble on his chin, a long scar extended from his right eye down almost below his right ear.

"Yeah, boss," answered the man. He listened as the proprietor whispered some instructions. "Sure," he said, after listening to the owner. Then he quickly moved through the door into the main store, out the entrance, and onto the large porch. He quickly glanced back left and then to the right. Then he saw the big man that the boss had told him about. He was on a gray mule and had started back south. The tall, thin man quickly went over to a brown mare that was tied up on the hitching rail. As he inserted his left foot into the stirrup and threw his right leg over the old, worn saddle, he could think of only one thing — that guy could cause us to hang.

Wilburn, still angry and still upset about the murder of his father, hardly noticed where he was going. With tears in his eyes, he finally looked up. Not far ahead was a creek that probably ran back to the river. A rough bridge, about fifteen feet long, had been built across the creek. Although still upset, Wilburn realized that he had not eaten that day.

"Ole mule, need to stop and eat som'in," he said and dismounted. He reached for the sack of food that Sarah had prepared for him. There were still a few items in the bag. He tied the mule to the railing of the bridge and then began to carefully move from the bridge down the incline to the creek below. The creek was almost a foot deep and the water looked to be acceptable to drink.

Wilburn moved just under the bridge and sat down on a piece of an old log that had been carried there by the water at some time. He reached for the sack and what was left of the food. There were three or four old biscuits and some smoked ham. After discarding two of the biscuits that had mold on them, he inserting some ham between the biscuit halves to create two small sandwiches.

He got his old tin coffee cup and dipped it into the clear water to fill it. I guess I had better offer thanks to the Lord for the food, Wilburn thought. He sat there for a minute or two before starting his prayer. He again thought about his deceased pa. How could any man take on his pa? It had to be two or three men anyway. He again thought about the storeowner that he had confronted earlier. He was sure that this guy knew something. There was guilt all over his face.

Wilburn bowed his head and began to pray. He thanked God for his Christian pa and for raising him like he did. He prayed for the family back in Bluffton — especially Sarah, his ma. He finished the prayer by thanking the Lord for his food. As he bit into the dry biscuit, he noticed that the mule made that characteristic sound, as if clearing his throat.

He glanced to his left and saw a figure coming at him with a knife. Wilburn quickly jerked back, and the knife narrowly missed his rib cage. His left hand instinctively went out to the assailant's upper arm, holding the moving knife. A second later, Wilburn used his right hand to grasp the wrist of the assailant. Then he jerked both of his hands toward him. The man's forearm hit against his knee; however, his upper arm and wrist continued to move towards Wilburn. He heard a loud crack and a scream, as a bone broke and ripped through muscle and flesh.

Leaning backward, Wilburn threw his entire weight forward, causing the screaming man to pitch forward into the shallow creek. Wilburn quickly released the man's shattered arm and went for his head. He aggressively forced the man's whole body under the water. Even in deep pain, the man struggled to escape the watery grave. But Wilburn's strong hands kept the man's head in the water, plunging it into the gravel at the bottom of the stream.

Just before the man quit struggling, Wilburn pulled the man's head up. He was out of breath, choking, and coughing. The man's arm was now bent in the wrong direction.

"Now, before we send you on to hell, do you want to tell me about my pa and who's involved, or do you need another long drink of water?" asked Wilburn as he examined the man's face.

"No — please. It was Roland."

"And who is Roland?" Wilburn asked, pushing the man's head beneath the water again. After another twenty seconds or so, grasping the man's hair, Wilburn jerked the man's head up above the water. "I'm waiting," he impatiently said.

"He owns the store. He sent me after you, while ago," the man said, gasping for air.

"How many were involved in my pa's murder?" Wilburn shouted at the man.

"Three — were three of us, but Roland planned it and sold all your pa's belongings."

Wilburn arrived at the sheriff's office in less than an hour, riding the mule and leading the brown mare. The man who had tried to kill him was lying on his stomach, over the saddle. A rope tied around the man's neck went beneath the belly of the horse and around to where it was tied to the man's feet on the other side. The compound fractured arm hung limply toward the ground. The captive cried out in pain most of the time during the trip to the sheriff's office.

After taking the man's confession, the deputy sheriff and Wilburn went to arrest the storeowner. Once the sheriff had handcuffed him, he walked over to the new cash register, took out one hundred and fifty dollars, and gave it to Wilburn.

"That'll help your loss," he said.

Earlier, the sheriff had asked if Wilburn wanted to visit the burial site of his father. Now, he asked him again.

"I guess not. You said it would be one of several unmarked graves, so I guess I will just start back to Bluffton. Course, I believe Pa's already in heaven anyway," explained Wilburn, extending his hand toward the deputy sheriff.

"Thanks, for helping us solve the murder — and ridding Pine Bluff of such vermin. If you like, I could send you a letter and tell you when the hanging will take place — probably less'n a month," suggested the deputy.

"No, that's okay. Just do a good job of it," said Wilburn as he walked back to the mule.

For most of the trip home, Wilburn thought about what he would say to the family about John. He knew that it would really be hard on Sarah and the girls. He also realized that he would now be the head of the family.

Although the mule was slow, Wilburn wasted little time getting home. Knowing that the family was really worried, he made it back to Seth's home by the first of September. When he arrived, he found no one at home. He started south, assuming the family was at the new building site. When he arrived there, he found all the family working, including Seth and Allie. He was shocked at the progress the group had made. All four walls of the log home were in place. From a distance, it appeared that the men had done a good job.

Someone looked up to see Wilburn and yelled to the family. Dropping what they were doing, everyone started back toward Wilburn as he approached. As Wilburn watched them, he noticed the concerned and worried look on their faces on not seeing John. He was sure that most of them now realized that if he had any news, it would not be good news.

"What about John?" Sarah called out even before she got close to Wilburn.

He dismounted from the mule and started toward his ma. She began to cry before he reached her. Wilburn reached out his arms and pulled Sarah close. Watching him, she already knew the answer.

"Pa will not be coming home," he said, as he slowly moved Sarah to one side. The girls immediately broke out crying. "He was bushwhacked while coming home. They've caught the guilty parties and they will hang for the crime. The wagon, oxen, furniture — everything was taken and sold."

He told them that the sheriff have given him one hundred and fifty dollars that he had taken from one of the men.

"That will replace what we lost — but we can't replace p- p-pa," Wilburn's voice broke as he finished his explanation.

Sarah was crying, with her head on Wilburn's chest.

"Pa was buried in a proper grave," Wilburn lied as he composed himself.

"It's close to suppertime; lets all go back to the house for the rest of the evening," Allie said, glancing around at the teary-eyed group.

"I agree," said William. "We need a rest."

David had already turned to go back and get the ox team that they had used to drag the heavy logs up to the building site. As he walked, he thought about his pa and what a great job that he had done in providing for his family. The move to Arkansas itself was just another effort on his part to provide a better life for them.

David thought, why does a good Christian man, one who loves his family, have to die at the hands of outlaws? They had prayed everyday for his pa. Where was the God that they all prayed to so much?

After David had reached the ox team, he grabbed the heavy iron yoke ring and pulled. The team started following him as he moved over to the field wagon. There he hooked the team to the wagon. He boarded the wagon and directed the oxen back to where the family waited.

William helped the women board the wagon, and then he and his other two brothers, along with Seth, climbed into the wagon, while Wilburn rode the mule back to Seth's home. After a delicious supper, the men went into the living room. They had a lot of questions to ask Wilburn about their pa's death.

"Men, long as the women are not here, I will answer your questions about pa's death — but when one of them comes in — no more. Don't want them to know the gory details."

Over the next half hour, Wilburn described his trip and the people he talked to about John. The men interrupted him several times, asking specific questions about the events surrounding his search and John's death. When David asked how the sheriff ever found the assailant, he paused, not wanting to relate everything — at least not yet.

He said the sheriff had a confession by one of the outlaws. He explained that the confession led to the arrest of a storeowner who had planned the murder and sold the family's furniture. He finally related that when the sheriff arrested the storeowner, he took the one hundred and fifty dollars from the man's cash register and gave it to him.

Although there were other questions, Wilburn closed the conversation when the ladies finished the kitchen cleanup. Wanting to avoid further discussion about John's death, Wilburn began to inquire about the construction of the new house. The womenfolk, still in shock, took little part in the conversation.

Sarah soon excused herself, indicating that she was tired and ready for bed. The twins went into their mom's bedroom to console her one last time before she went to bed, and the men retired to the front porch.

Assuming his new role as head of the family, Wilburn turned to Seth.

"Can we finish the home — roof and outside — before cold weather?"

"I think so," replied Seth, who had said very little since realizing that he had lost his brother. "Wilburn, you, and even the mule, will provide a lot of extra help. We still have to cut trees for the roof. The boys say that you are good with the ax, and we have more help now than when we built our home."

Seth told Wilburn that they had used the money that John gave him to make a down payment on land through the bank at Danville.

"We also brought back lime, nails, and other items that we will need," he said. "Actually, we are in good shape."

"Who did your fireplace and chimney?" Wilburn asked Seth.

"Aw, I did it, with neighbors' help. If ya'll carry and place the rocks, I can do that fer you."

By December, the home was finished. A barn, chicken house, smokehouse, and the outhouse were also completed.

Chapter 13

The First Battle

EXCEPT FOR LINGERING MEMORIES of John, the Loflands had a good Christmas in the new log home. Junior cut a small, pine tree that was soon decorated with homemade ornaments. The colored pinecones really added to the tree. Sarah and Allie produced a delicious Christmas meal, topped off by a huge, wild turkey that David had just killed. With Rachel's special dressing and a variety of vegetables, everyone ate too much. There was no gift exchange between family members, but there was a special time of singing Christmas carols while Seth played his violin.

Allie brought out one of her specialties, bread pudding, late on Christmas evening. Afterwards, Seth produced his grandfather's old family Bible. The older man read the Christmas story from the second chapter of Luke. After the reading, Seth asked all to bow their heads in prayer. He thanked God for the entire Lofland family and for his care. He almost broke down crying when he mentioned John — especially when he said that he knew John was in heaven. David could also hear his ma start to cry when Seth referred to John.

"We all can see how the Lord has blessed our family — and Uncle Seth and Aunt Allie," Sarah said after the prayer, wiping her eyes. Everyone silently listened. "Let's pray that in the coming year, the Lord will continue to keep his hands on us."

When everyone had gone to bed, and Junior had fallen asleep in the double bed he shared with David, David lay in the bed thinking. He thought about the festive and enjoyable Christmas Day. It could have only been better if his pa had been there. And then he remembered Lillie — she would have made it more wonderful. He remembered his ma's prayer. Once again she — and the others, he guessed — believed that God had really blessed the Lofland family over the past year.

That was hard to believe, thought David. Becky had been pregnant, and she had tried to kill herself, and even worse, their beloved pa had been brutally murdered — and the team of oxen and the wagon loaded with furniture had been stolen. If this was God's will, and an example of his care, David wondered what it would be like if God was against them! And then a thought — maybe we need a fat preacher here to pray for us. Finally, David drifted off into a troubled sleep.

~~~

1860 had been a presidential election year. By then, even the least informed of the American people realized that the country was nearing a serious crisis. Several Southern states had seceded from the Union in the latter months of the Buchanan administration. The action taken by the seceded states was not directed against the Buchanan government; rather, it was the result of the 1860 presidential election. A man from Illinois, a member of the new Republican Party, had been elected president.

Abraham Lincoln had not been on the Arkansas presidential ballot or on any Southern states' ballot. However, there were three candidates on the Arkansas ballot, as with most of the Southern states. The Southern Democratic Party's candidate was John Breckenridge, the sitting vice president. A second candidate from the state of Illinois was on the Arkansas ballot. This was Senator Stephen Douglas, who represented the northern wing of the Democratic Party. Finally, a separate third-party candidate, John Bell, represented the Constitutional Party. Breckenridge won in Arkansas; however, since the state's vote was split among the three hopefuls, Lincoln won the national vote with a minority decision. Since the Republican Party voiced serious concerns about the existence of slavery — though constitutional — it got little support in the South.

The Southern states, relatively sure how a Lincoln presidency might affect them, would decide to secede before he took office. While Arkansas was one of the last states to secede, it and ten other states would eventually form a new government in Montgomery, Alabama — the Confederate States of America. The question now for the Southern people was, what would happen if Lincoln used force against the South? What would happen if the Federal army invaded the South?

The year 1860 was also the first year that the Loflands harvested a cotton crop. The cleared bottomland near the Fourche River proved to be as fertile as Seth had predicted. The last of the large tree stumps were removed from the fields near the new home, although Wilburn often wondered how long the older oxen could continue pulling out the huge stumps. The Loflands planted thirty acres in cotton and five more in corn. The crop that fall exceeded all their expectations — especially with cotton selling over fourteen cents per pound.

~~~

On Tuesday, July 23, 1861, Wilburn sent David to Bluffton to visit with Lem Bryant, the blacksmith/harness shop owner who also raised horses and mules. Previously, Lem had told Wilburn that he had a good team of mules for sale. Wilburn was considering using mules over oxen to plow the fertile river bottom soil. He also knew that the oxen were now quite old.

David arrived in town about 10:00 a.m. He dismounted from the mule and went into the big building that housed Lem's thriving business. It sounded like a fight was taking place near the far end of the building. When he got to the gathered men, David realized that it was not a fight, but instead, something interesting that all the men had heard. They were all obviously excited. James Ogden, another farmer, turned when David got to the group and asked what David thought about it.

"What you talking 'bout?" said David, parting his hands as if to say, I haven't been informed.

"You hadn't heard, Dave?" Lem asked in a surprised manner.

"Ferrell had his tenth kid?" replied David as everyone broke out laughing.

Ferrell, whose wife was usually pregnant, had already given birth to nine children.

"We's defeated the cocky Yankees rite on Washington's doorstep. Place called Manasses, near a creek called Bull Run. Whupped them and sent them cowardly running back to Washington. They say we could have captured Washington and the railsplitter."

"They talkin' 'bout one of our generals, Stonewall Johnson."

"I believe it was Jackson, not Johnson," interrupted Ray Hunnicutt.

"'Nother was Johnson. Killed right smart number of 'em too."

"Did they surrender?" asked David, hoping the war was already over.

"Naw, didn't give up yet. Shows what us durn Southerds can do even if we'uns are outnumbered."

"What's really funny is the high–falutin' folks from Washington all came down for a picnic to watch the Yankees beat us. Now they's all back in Washington hiding behind the outhouse," related Kirk Breed, one of the farmers that attended church with David.

"Gosh — who would have believed it was so easy," said David. "Well, hav'ta tell the boys 'bout this."

He and a couple other men turned and walked to the big door and out on the street. As he did, he almost ran into Brother Turner, the pastor at Community Church.

"Sorry, Brother Turner; wasn't paying attention after hearing 'bout the big victory."

"I understand, David. Everyone is excited over the victory, but we need to remember, there are many more battles to come and we may not win them all. How is the folks?"

"They are fine; ma jest got over the congestion, but she's doing better."

"Good. We'll be in prayer for her. See you David," the pastor said as he walked down the street.

David thought, 'nother one of those preachers being friendly so's we fill the offering plate. Why don't he work like the rest of us? Got those lily-white hands — probably never had a blister or a cut on his hands.

I believe I could fool people well enough to be a preacher, David thought. Parson Lofland sounds good, but maybe I'd need to gain some weight. Course, I would need to have the Lord bless me with the prettiest girl in Yell County. He stopped, and thought, I didn't even talk to Lem 'bout the mule team. He turned around and started back to the blacksmith shop. When David walked into the business, Lem was already working on a new horse harness.

"Howdy ag'in, Dave," said Lem, looking up from hammering a brad into place.

"Lem, ready to sell that team of mules?" David asked, glancing around the shop.

"You bet, and a good team, I might add. My son was thinking 'bout gettin' 'em — course, I'd 'lowed him to have 'em much cheaper. But he decided to join the army."

"Lem, Brad wasn't in that battle ya'll's talking about, was he?"

Lem pulled out a twist of tobacco and bit off a sizable amount. "No, he joined at Danville, and they sent him over to Dardanelle to train. Feller name of Harvell is training the men. Oh, he likes it; course, he'd do anything if'n it allowed him to shoot a gun. Let me finish this other brad and we'll go look at the mules."

"You know, Lem, I've been thinking about joining up with the army. Feller could save his money and maybe buy some land," explained David.

"You not 'bout to marry, are you, Dave?" Lem said as he inserted a new brad in a hole of the harness.

"No way," David laughed. "Doubt if I ever get married — can't find no one that would have me." He laughed again. As Lem also laughed, David thought, a preacher man stole the woman I love.

The mules were a fine-looking team. David, who was good with any work animals, mules or oxen, knew they were worth sixteen dollars.

"You gonna take 'em today?" Lem asked.

"Yeah. Wilburn said if I liked 'em to go ahead and pay you and bring 'em home." He counted out the money carefully as Lem watched.

"Hey, ya'll want a cookie?"

David turned around to see an attractive lady, possibly eighteen or nineteen years of age. Lem looked at the lady, reached over to the plate that she was holding, and took two chocolate cookies. As the lady extended the plate toward David, Lem placed his hand on her shoulder.

"Abbie Sue, this is Dave Lofland; they lives out south of here. Dave, Abbie Sue is my niece; she lives over at Danville — visiting with us."

David extended his hand to the girl's small, extended hand. As he did, he noticed her smile, her pretty teeth, and the beautiful, light brown hair that hung down to her shoulders. No doubt, this girl was beautiful.

"Dave has just bought a mule team off me today," Lem said. "Wait, Dave, and I'll bring them around and through the barn." He left, walking toward the back door.

"Abbie Sue, you come to Bluffton often?" asked a slightly nervous David.

The girl smiled and glanced back toward the end of the barn. "Maybe once or twice a year. I spent a lot of the summers here with Uncle Lem and Aunt Joice when I was young. Some of my favorite times were here in Bluffton," explained the attractive girl.

"You're not from here, are you, David?" she asked.

"No, I was born in North Carolina and raised in Tennessee. We came here 'bout six months ago," he said, looking back for Lem.

Lem had now brought the mules into the big barn. When David saw Lem and the mules, he turned to Abbie Sue.

"Hope we can visit again sometime, Abbie Sue; sure good to meet you."

"Good to meet you, David. Good-bye," she said as David

walked into the barn section of the business.

Riding home on the mule and leading the new team, David thought about the day. The war had begun, and the South had won the initial battle, but the war didn't end. There would be more battles, probably some in Arkansas. Should he join and defend his new state, as well as the other two states that he had lived in, North Carolina and Tennessee? What about this new girl in town, Abbie Sue? Maybe not a Lillie, but she was no slouch either. He knew that he would see Abbie Sue again.

When David arrived at the new Lofland home, everyone quit their work to come out and look over the new residents.

"What we gonna call them, Ma?" asked David. "They are both females."

"Well, I had two twin aunts — probably why John and I had the twin girls. Their names were Belle and Nelle. I loved them both very much. Since the two brown mules look so much alike, let's name them Belle and Nelle; what do you think?"

The twin girls clapped and the boys showed their approval for the new names. Wilburn had been examining the mules while listening to the family's comments.

"Okay, Belle will be the one with the lighter brown face — she will be the left mule. Nelle, with a darker face, will be the right mule. Everyone agree?"

"I'd better write that down, so's I'll remember," countered Seth. Everyone laughed.

Chapter 14

A Slave?

THE COTTON CROP FROM the river bottomland was unbelievable. At twelve cents per pound, the Loflands should sell enough cotton to even pay off their loan at Chambers Bank in Danville. Everyone helped pick cotton in September. Seth, using the mules, drove the field wagon, which picked up the cotton at special places near the ends of the cotton rows. Once he had a full load of cotton, he would disconnect the loaded wagon and then hook the mule team up to the other wagon. After filling both wagons, Seth and Wilburn would drive the wagons to the Hunnicutt gin at Bluffton, with Seth using the oxen and Wilburn using the mules. Picking cotton continued while the wagons were taken to Bluffton. By mid-September, the fields were bare, the gin at Bluffton was busy, and the Loflands could finally rest.

One evening in late September, the Loflands relaxed and visited with Wilburn's girlfriend, Grace Mason. Sarah joined them after finishing the dishes. .

"We have worked awful hard this year, but we have paid most of our farm off. Let's remember that the Lord has really blessed the Lofland family this year," she said. "Maybe John has connections in heaven. Before we begin bragging on our great crop, don't forget that God is really responsible for our success. Don't you agree, William?"

"Sure do, Ma. Don't think any farmer in the Fourche Valley has done so well," Wilburn enthusiastically replied. "Ma, what you think 'bout us buying a slave or two? They would easily pay for themselves, and we could afford them," he asked, looking around at the others.

Sarah, who respected Wilburn even more, probably because he was so much like his father, usually listened to his point of view.

"Well, I don't know; you reckon your pa would have used slaves?" Sarah asked her oldest son.

Wilburn again looked around at the other family members for possible support.

"Yeah, I do, Ma. I know a lot of people see a moral problem with slavery but the Bible approves of slavery in both the Old and New Testament. They's Christian slave owners all over the South. Six or seven of our presidents have owned black slaves. I know, Northerners are opposed to slavery, but they are not farmers either."

David, who had previously discussed the use of slaves with Wilburn, had listened carefully to the discussion.

"I kind of agree, but what about the war? If we lose the war, will we still be allowed to keep any slaves that we buy? What you reckon, William?"

"Looks like we will win the war, all right, so any slaves we owned would be safe. But, there's still other things to be thought 'bout. One, I don't want to break up any black families if'n we buy slaves. Ya'll remember the slave auction at Memphis? Even be good to keep 'em together. If we git two slaves, it would be good to git two brothers, if possible."

"Makes sense, if possible; course, I don't know if they ever sell brothers together," replied Wilburn.

"Ya'll 'member the slave over at Perryville who murdered

his master — a preacher. That slave had a sister who was also owned by the preacher," stated David. Then he thought, the preacher man got what he deserved.

"Well, I'll check on the next auction at Dardanelle. If they have some young males, we will try to go over," Wilburn stated, looking at Sarah.

More than fifty people worshipped at the Community Church in Bluffton on Sunday. All the Loflands were in attendance, except for Allie, who had not been feeling well. David would not have gone to church, except that he hated to hurt his mother's feelings. After he arrived, he felt much better when he noticed Abbie Sue going up the church steps with her uncle, Lem Bryant. She wasn't aware that David was entering the church door behind her, and he took the opportunity to notice everything about her.

She was dressed in a beautiful, white dress that was trimmed in red. She wore a matching bonnet that was also trimmed in red. Her lipstick matched the red in her attire. The tight-fitting dress enhanced her tiny waist and ample bosom. Below her attractive bonnet, her carefully brushed hair hung below to her shoulders.

Once inside the church, the Lofland ladies moved toward the front to take a seat on the third row. Seth and the four brothers followed the women and took a seat behind the ladies on the fourth row. Last to go up the aisle, David sat down in the end seat. After glancing around the church, he noticed Abbie Sue sitting across the aisle, a row in front to him. At the same time, Abbie Sue happened to glance to her right at the Lofland women and then back to the men. David caught her eye and she smiled before turning back to face the song leader who had just moved to the podium.

"Hey, welcome everyone; hope you ain't worked too hard this week. We finished our pickin' like most of you'uns. Good to see the Loflands all here, 'cause they fill two rows." Several people laughed. "Let's turn to page 301, 'Lord, We Are Yours' — and all stand."

The song leader, Mack Holland, was also the owner of the general store. While he had no training in music, Mack had an excellent voice and frequently sang special music for the services. After two more songs, Mack asked everyone to turn to page 11, 'Bringing In The Sheaves.'

"After the last verse, would four of you men on the outside by the aisle come forward for our offering?"

David looked back behind him and noticed that he was one of the men by the aisle. At the end of the final verse, he got up and moved to the front of the pastor's pulpit. Three other men followed him. After a brief prayer by Pastor Turner, the four men took the wooden offering plates and each moved to one of the aisles.

As David handed the offering plate to the man on the outside of aisle two, he glanced at Abbie. She was looking at him. While he waited for the offering plate being passed by those sitting on her row, she again glanced at David, smiling. She has got a pretty smile, thought David. When the offering had been taken, one of the ushers placed the partially filled offering plates on the table in front of the pastor's pulpit. David and the other two men took their seats. He could not help looking over toward Abbie once more.

Pastor Turner, usually a soft-spoken man, always seemed to change the minute he got behind the pulpit. He was much louder and sometimes stuttered some. "Good morning, and what a day the Lord has given us today."

"Amen," someone said.

"Let's be in prayer for those who are suffering — especially Mrs. Hartford, who lost her mom this week. Would you please turn in your Bible to Leviticus? We are talking about giving or tithing today. But first, what does the Bible say about giving?"

David looked down his own row. Seth was already half asleep. David slightly slid forward in the seat, into a more comfortable position. He was also tired, after the coon hunt the night before.

"If you would turn to Leviticus, go to verse 30, and read with me, 'A tithe of everything from the land, whether grain from the soil or fruit from the trees, belongs to the Lord; it is holy to the Lord.' Neighbors, a tithe is ten percent. We are to give ten percent of our cotton, wheat, corn, cattle, hogs, or anything else that the Lord has blessed us with — maybe not the actual cotton or hog, but at least their worth. The question is — how much do we want to follow the Lord's word? No, we say, 'I can buy that new dining room table, or that new plow, or that prize bull. The Lord will understand, I'm sure, because the Browns have that nice table and ours is old.' Has the Lord really blessed you? If he has, repay him as he asks."

As David grew sleepier, he thought about what the preacher was saying. Sounds like the preacher himself may need a new table or a prize bull. He doesn't work hard like we do plowing and picking cotton. David slowly drifted off to sleep. He woke up when the pastor said, "Let's stand and turn to page 10, 'It Is Well With My Soul.'"

David sleepily got to his feet, after most of the people had already stood. Though quite drowsy, he hung on to the back of the seat in front of him and stayed upright. With the benediction, the people began to move to the main aisle and down toward the front door. Several people spoke to him and David muttered a hello. He walked back to the wagon, totally forgetting the attractive Abbie Sue, who was looking around for him.

As Wilburn drove the mule team and wagon, they talked about the preacher's sermon. Sarah was the first to voice her opposition now to purchasing a slave.

"We have done well with our crops. The Lord has blessed us with good health and good weather. I believe we need to forgo a slave and give the Lord a return on his blessing."

"Ma, believe you are right — I kin'a felt guilty today. We already got a new mule team and now we are 'bout to buy slave or two — I agree with you," stated Wilburn.

"Believe you right," agreed William.

"What about it, David?" Sarah asked, looking back at him.

"We give money to the church — probably much as anyone. What's the preacher going to do with the extra money? 'Sides, you can teach a slave 'bout God."

"I agree with David," said Junior, looking at Sarah. "We gonna be dead if we continue the twelve-hour days. We need help, especially since Wilburn is considering marrying Grace."

The idea of purchasing a slave was soon forgotten, since only David and Junior were in favor of it.

Chapter 15

A Tough Decision

February - 1862

FEBRUARY WAS NOT AS cold as previous winters. However, it was still cold enough to welcome the heat that could be soaked up from the big fireplace. That's what the Lofland family was doing one Friday in mid February as they gathered in the big living room. Only David had chosen not to join the family. Instead, he sat alone at the dining room table, appearing to be preoccupied with something.

Everyone knew that David was not happy. The other boys had noticed that he was short-tempered and rather irritable. On one recent occasion, he had hit the Jersey cow with a two-by-four board, after the cow kicked the milk bucket over on the ground.

Nothing seemed to hold his attention anymore. He and Junior had gone bear hunting a couple of times, but even the weekly coon hunts were no longer interesting. Since it was winter, there was little serious farming to do, so that added to the restlessness he felt. He had not even gone to church much lately, much to Sarah's disappointment.

David also didn't talk much anymore. When he did talk, it was about joining the Confederate Army. No one encouraged him to join the army, but some wondered if getting away for a while might do him good.

Sarah had noticed that he had lost weight over the past six months. She was so concerned about her son that she had spoken to the pastor about him.

And David was having trouble sleeping. He still occasionally thought about Lillie, including wondering if she had children yet. He also wondered if he would ever get back to Hickory Flats. He hadn't seen Abbie Sue since the previous fall. She had returned to her home in Danville not long after David had last seen her at Community Church. The severe winter months of 1861 played a part due to the unusual amount of snow and ice. Travel was difficult, especially over Mount George. However, there was more; David had began to dwell even more on his past problems, which in turn caused even more depression.

Now, as David pondered his future, Sarah quietly got up and came into the dining room. She sat down across the table from him and placed her hand on his arm.

"You all right, son?" she asked.

"Yeah, I'm fine, Ma. Just thinking."

"Mind if I ask what about?" Sarah asked, studying his face.

"Ma, I'm going to join the army," he said after a pause. "They need help, and since its winter, I don't have many chores to do; Junior can do them. Would you give me your approval?"

"Dave, you don't need my approval now," she said, looking at his unhappy face. "You are a man. But, I would give you my approval if you would do one thing first for me."

"What's that, Ma?" questioned David, looking at Sarah for the first time.

"Would you first talk to Pastor Turner before you leave?" she softly asked.

He looked back at her. He really loved his ma, and he knew that she had worked so hard since his pa had died. He knew that he would meet her request, out of respect, if nothing more.

"Guess so, Ma," he replied.

"When you going, son?" she asked, still looking at his troubled face.

He glanced back toward the living room, where everyone had laughed about something.

"Day after tomorrow, if it's all right?" David replied, glancing down at his callused hands.

"Would you talk with the pastor when you go to Danville?" Sarah asked, with concern in her voice. "He won't try to talk you out of it."

"Okay, Ma. I would do it for you."

"Thank you, son. I will have your clothes ready day after tomorrow."

The following day, everyone heard about David's decision. No doubt, all family members hated to see him join the army; yet, all realized that David was not happy. As Wilburn and William fed the oxen, mules, and pigs, they had an opportunity to talk about David's decision.

"Thing that worries me is that the Federals seem to be winning now. Feller by name of Grant has forced a Confederate fort in Tennessee to surrender. Fifteen hundred Rebs were taken prisoner. Worst thing is death, but to be taken prisoner is always a possibility," Wilburn said.

"Nothing we can say that would help, so guess we will have to live with it," replied William. "He may really like it."

The good-byes were difficult for the family. The womenfolk, especially Sarah, all showed tears as he prepared to go. The men had worried looks on their faces. Wilburn had tried to get David to let them take him to Danville in the wagon, but he said he would rather ride the old gray mule and leave it at the blacksmith shop for them.

"Dave, we don't need that old mule anymore, with the new, young team that we just bought. Actually, he don't get along very well with the new mules anyway. Take him and then sell him at Jake's Blacksmith Shop in Danville — even at a giveaway price. That will give you some extra money to buy new shoes or som'in."

As he mounted the old mule, Sarah came up close near his leg.

"Don't forget to stop on your way and see the preacher," she whispered as she patted his thigh with her hand. "Love ya."

"Love ya, Ma."

David slightly nudged the old mule with his heel as several good-byes were called out to him.

~~~

When David arrived at Pastor Turner's home, he knocked a couple of times before the preacher opened the door. When he saw the young man standing there, he extended his hand in welcome.

"Hello, Dave. Good to see you; come in."

David had never been in the pastor's home. He was surprised that the furnishings in the home were only average, and maybe even less impressive than in the new Lofland home. Mrs. Turner entered the room with a friendly smile.

"Morning, David. Would you like coffee?" she asked.

"Guess not, ma'am," he replied. "I started drinking coffee this morning at 5:00 a.m., but thank you."

"Well, I'll be out back washing clothes, so holler if you need me, Al," she said and left the room to go back into the kitchen.

The pastor had taken a seat in a rocking chair beside David.

"I guess you're on your way to Danville," he said, looking at the young man.

Wonder if he's going to try to talk me outta it, thought David.

"Yeah, want to get their 'fore dark," he said, thinking, maybe he won't talk so long if he knows I need to leave early.

Sensing that David was somewhat uncomfortable about their conversation, the pastor assured him that they could talk and have a prayer in no more than fifteen minutes.

"David, I will be brief, but I will also get to the point. Your ma is somewhat concerned about your faith in God. Now, she may be wrong, but she even wonders if you continue to be a believer. And David, we know how mothers are; they worry about the least things. However, in this case — you going off to war — she is even more worried about your faith. We know death is a possibility in war. We all know what happened at Pea Ridge. I must ask you, as your pastor, how you feel about some things. Is that okay?"

"Al right," he answered in a slow, uncomfortable manner.

"David, do you believe in a God? The Creator of the universe? A God that sees our every move? A God who wants only the best for us? A God that blesses us? Even a God who sent his son to die for us?" the preacher asked, intently looking at David.

There was a pause, as if David was composing an answer to the questions.

"Sure have doubts. Maybe a creator, but as for one that helps us, or makes us happy, or allows our desires and wishes to come true — I doubt that. I was raised to read the Bible and to pray and to obey the words of God or Jesus. I'm not a holy person, but I'm not a mean person either. Brother Turner, I've seen very little good come my way for the last year or so," he said, looking the pastor in the eye.

"In what way?" asked the pastor, carefully studying David.

"Well, we lost little Joe, our brother. I lost a girlfriend who I really loved. We lost pa. My own sister tried to drown herself because the family shamed her so much over getting pregnant."

David's voice rose as he made his case.

"Preacher, that's a lot to happen in one family in less than a year. Somebody may be getting blessed, but it's not me. If there is a God up there, somebody needs to remind him that we are not the meanest family in Arkansas."

David was now angrily glaring at the pastor, as if angry at him as well.

"Well, David, lots has happened in your family, but much of it is God's will," the pastor said, looking from his folded hands into David's eyes. And then David lost it.

"That's all I hear — God's will! It's God's will — always the crutch you people use. If that's the case, why doesn't he love us enough to help save us from some of the evil in the world?" David said, thinking about the bad things he'd seen or heard about happening to others as well. "What about the poor, starving Indians and Africans I saw being sold on the slave block? What about the preacher I heard about who was raping a young black girl? Her brother, a slave, killed the man, and he will hang. Is God blessing them?"

He had stood up while he was talking, and now he reached for the doorknob.

"Don't want to hear anymore of this mumbo jumbo," he said indignantly.

"Wait, David, just a minute."

The door slammed as David left the pastor's home. He heard Pastor Turner open the door, but David ignored him and walked on toward the mule. Later, a couple of his acquaintances waved as David rode out of town toward Danville. They were surprised that he never waved back at them.

It was late when David got in sight of Danville, so he decided to camp out near the south edge of town below Mount George. He had thought about the conversation with the pastor for most of the trip. While he was sure that he had expressed himself the way that he intended, he also felt guilty about his disrespectful and abrupt departure. The pastor had been able to say very little and David felt bad about that. He hoped that the pastor would not tell everything to his ma.

~~~

After a poor night's sleep, David was up early and ready to finish his journey. Within twenty minutes, he had reached Danville. The town of about two hundred and fifty people was one of the fastest-growing towns in the area. Like Bluffton, Danville had a cotton gin. It had two general stores, Jake's Blacksmith Shop, a small restaurant, and Chambers Bank. There was also a gristmill along the Petit Jean River north of town.

Having been to Danville several times, David knew the town quite well. The blacksmith shop was north of Main Street not far from the river. The courthouse was almost directly across the street from the blacksmith shop. He decided to go into the courthouse first and check on induction procedures.

When he entered the door, he saw a sign up ahead at the end of the hall. The sign simply read, "Army Sign Up," and an arrow pointed down a long hall to the right. He reached the door of the office and noticed three other men standing in line in front of a worn desk. When he saw David, the tired-looking man behind the desk took off his glasses and rubbed his eyes. This was the eleventh man to sign up already this morning. The first man in the line was signing a paper. When he finished, he handed it back to the official at the desk.

"Go over to that door, if you would," requested the official. When the soldier-to-be got to the door, an attractive young lady suddenly opened it. It was Abbie Sue. She invited the man into the office. She had not noticed David waiting in line at the desk.

David signed a piece of paper stating that he was at least eighteen years of age, and then waited for his turn to go to the office that the others had entered. The door again opened after he had waited about ten minutes. Abbie Sue was completely surprised to see David standing there.

"Going to join up?" she asked, regaining her composure and smiling at David.

"No, I came to ask you for a date," he said, trying to keep from laughing. Then she realized it was a joke. Both laughed.

"It is good to see you again," she said, motioning for him to sit down. "Let's complete the paperwork, and then maybe we will have time to talk."

David completed three induction papers while asking several questions about the papers. After finishing the last one, he looked over at Abbie, who was filing some papers.

"You work for the army?"

"No, I work for Yell County," she said, turning back to face David and taking his last page. "That involves inducting county men into the military. You will need to go down to Room 101, where you will talk to an officer about training and dates of departure," Abbie said as she halfway turned around.

"Abbie, could I possibly see you this evening?" he cautiously asked.

She waited a few seconds before answering.

"David, I didn't hear anymore from you after we met, or since that time in Bluffton. Since then, I guess I would say I've been spoken for — actually a fiancée. We are to be married in August. I'm sorry, but I hope we can still be friends."

"Oh — well," David said, ducking his head in embarrassment. "Congratulations; hope you will be happy. I need to go to Room 101."

"Thank you, David, and may God bless and care for you as you defend our country," she replied, smiling at him.

As he walked down to Room 101, David thought, just another slap in the face. What's next? When he got to the room, a soldier, dressed in Confederate gray, opened the door to leave the office.

"Come in and sit down," he said, motioning with his right hand, without looking at David. "Be right back."

David stepped into the office, looked around, and took a seat near a large desk. On the wall was a picture of the new president, Jefferson Davis. In the corner behind the desk was the new national flag. The officer soon returned, holding several papers. As he moved behind the desk, he repositioned a picture on his desk.

"My fiancée works in the office you just came from," he said. "You probably talked to her."

Then David noticed the picture. It was Abbie Sue.

"Yeah, I had met her once earlier. She is an attractive lady," he said, still looking at the picture on the desk.

"Sure is. Thanks."

The officer spent the next hour explaining what procedure David would go through while preparing for military training.

"Any questions I might answer at this point?" the officer asked.

"No. Probably have some later."

"Let me ask you a question; are you ready today?" the officer asked, looking carefully at David. "What I mean is we have a group leaving tomorrow for training at Sulfur Springs. If you prefer to wait, another group will go 'bout a week of today."

"I'll go tomorrow, if it's okay," David replied.

The officer picked up another paper and began to write. "Is there one 'F' or two 'F's in Lofland?"

"Only one, sir," he replied, thinking he might as well start with military protocol.

~~~

The military wagon left at 8:00 a.m. the next morning for Sulfur Springs, a Confederate military training camp. Before long the men on board the wagon began to visit and develop friendships. Glen Lumry, a twenty-year-old farm boy from Briggsville, turned out to be the clown of the group. Lum, as his close friends referred to him, kept everyone laughing with his comments and criticism. Before long, David and Lum were conversing like old friends. David thought, I am gonna really like this guy; he is funny as everything but he is also very smart. Unknown to David, Lum also really liked him.

Chapter 16

Camp Sulfur Springs

July 1862

THE CAMP WAS NOT as impressive as the men had expected. There was a small shed for some purpose and a huge, reasonably level pastureland. Several tents had already been erected. Outside of a small flagpole, nothing else was on the old, pasture.

The training was both boring and interesting. The country boys from Yell County were all hunters, and shooting the different caliber muskets was enjoyable as well as competitive. Anyone that could hit the red, six-inch bulls-eye was lauded and praised by the other marksmen. And conversely, the poor marksmen were sometimes openly criticized, though usually in a humorous manner.

When one man missed the target altogether, Lum yelled, "Good shot; you killed the captain's horse, Alice." When another soldier hit the ground in front of the target, Lum turned to the disappointed shooter and said, "If we get hungry, you can kill ground squirrels for us." As usual, this brought laughter.

The comedian was finally able to break through to David, after watching him fire the 50-caliber musket. "Lofland, you and I will be side by side in battle. You shoot and kill Yankees, and I will load your gun and write letters to your girlfriend."

Before long, Lum and "Blue," a nickname Lum gave to David because of the color of his eyes, became fast friends. A third soldier was added to the friendship when the two men got to know a short, skinny man that weighed about one hundred and ten pounds. Though no athlete with any special skills of any kind, Murlan Skidoff drew David and Lum's attention because of some of the strange accomplishments he could do. He could hang from a limb by his hands for an unbelievable time. He could also climb a tree faster than anyone they had ever seen.

"If he had a bushy tail, I would be sure he was half squirrel," retorted Lum.

With his slender physique, Murlan could squeeze through the smallest opening.

"You will come in handy — 'specially if we need you to sneak in a hen house and catch us some fried chicken," Lum said, looking at Murlan. "Only thing, you couldn't carry a stolen watermelon bigger an onion. Course Blue can carry the big melon while I bring the salt and spoons," Lum surmised, smiling at David.

When Lum got wound up, he would go on for minutes. "What kind of name is Murlan, Chaldean? As the official general from Yell County, I hereby change your handle to Squirrel — till death do ya part — here, have an acorn."

Both David and Murlan, hence Squirrel, were amazed at Lum's imagination. He did bring a lot of humor into their days of drudgery in the training camp.

The training officer was a man named Leonard Spoke. Spoke, who Lum quickly renamed Spook, was sent to the camp through Governor Rector's office in Little Rock. Three other members of the state militia came with Captain Spoke. While Spoke was not of a military background, he apparently believed that he had written the book on military procedure. The entire first hour or so of training was spent on learning how to salute properly. It seemed that the men had some difficulty in reaching Spoke's level of proficiency. The officer, a former resident of Alabama, finally asked the men to sit down on the grass.

"We gonna learn the various commands that a soldier should know," he said with a lifted chin. "First is 'Attention.' On that command, you should stand straight, tall, and be erect.

"Squirrel, you erect yet?" David heard Lum whisper.

"Your chin should be up and firm, with your eyes straight ahead. No glancing to either side, even for hours. You will stand there with your hands hanging down beside your legs. A second command is 'At Ease.' When given this command, you will quickly spread you feet to the width of your shoulders and clasp your hands together behind your back while you relax. A third command is, 'About Face,' or quickly turn around backwards. You will execute this command by pivoting on your right foot."

He showed the men how to make the move. "Then another command, 'Forward, March,'— you push off on the right foot and lead with the left foot. Next command is, 'Halt' — you stop your march. Now, let me have five men arm's length apart, and others lined up behind each man."

There were now five men in a line, with four men behind each man, totaling twenty men in all. The captain moved over to the side and looked back over the five lines of man. "Forward, March."

After an hour of marching, the captain called, "Halt," and dismissed the men for lunch. As the men ate their prepared lunch of beans and fried potatoes, they discussed the morning activities.

"General Spook is a real jerk. The best command that he gave all morning was, 'About Face,' because I was so tired looking at his face," Lum said as he took a drink of water. "That guy was so excited that I wanted to say, General, 'At Ease,' please."

The others laughed.

"I know we will march a lot, especially when we go into battle, but why are we marching in circles?" asked David, putting his plate on the ground.

"Squirrel, you get drunk going in circles?" Lum asked.

"Naw, I'm still trying to 'member how to salute," replied Murlan.

"Yeah, I noticed you stuck a finger in your eye once," joked Lum.

Three other men walked by and spoke to the men.

"We ain't seen nothin' yet; we will get muskets to carry after lunch, and then the fun will begin. A musket will weigh fifteen pounds. You notice that after 'bout three hours," David said, looking back toward the captain.

"I wonder how long we gonna be here training? According to some, the Yankees are winning over in Tennessee. They may need us sooner than you think," Squirrel said.

The afternoon went by in a hurry, as the members of the 24th Regiment marched and countermarched. After the tired threesome lay down in their blankets for nightfall, there was more talk about the training.

"Ya'll raw in the crotch? Don't think I have any skin left there — all out there in the pasture somewhere. Couple of days, I won't be able to walk. Man, I'm sore," David said, rubbing himself.

"I hope that the Spook is so sore he has to sleep standing up," countered Lum. "Hey, got an idea; what if Spook lost a shoe overnight? Wouldn't it be interesting to see him in only one shoe right after reveille?" Lum asked, smiling.

"You think he's going to lose a shoe overnight?" David said, pulling up his blanket.

"No, but it might disappear. I could distract him while Squirrel crawled under his tent and stole his shoe," Lum replied.

"How'ed you distract him?" David asked, now interested.

"You in, Squirrel?" Lum asked, speaking to the smaller friend.

"If'n you do a good job of getting him outside his tent," replied Squirrel.

"Okay, Squirrel, get your shoes on. Slip outside and over to Spook's tent — the backside. I'm going to go outside and act like I'm choking. David will be trying to help me," Lum said, grinning.

"After he comes out to check on me, you go under his tent and get a shoe. Then throw the shoe in those high weeds behind the storage shed and come on around to observe the show."

Squirrel was already pulling his pants on, and David started to put his pants on as well.

"No, we going out in underwear. Remember, I'm choking," Lum said, "Got to look real."

"What you supposed to be choking on?" David asked, smiling.

"Oh — what about plug of tobacco?" said Lum.

Within ten minutes, Squirrel looked out the tent and around the camp. No one was moving. He quietly walked toward the captain's tent, which was about twenty yards away. It appeared that the officer had gone to sleep. He now awaited the appearance of his two friends. A loud noise soon came from the trio's tent. Lum then came out of the tent, making a loud gagging noise and holding his throat.

"Are you choking?" shouted David. "You choking?"

As usual, Lum was hamming it up and enjoying every bit of it. Five or six other concerned soldiers were already outside their tents, anxiously watching. Suddenly, out of his tent came the captain, pulling up his pants.

"What happened? What's going on?"

As Squirrel crawled under the captain's tent, he heard David shouting, "He's choked on a plug of tobacco."

David was slapping Lum hard on the back. Two or three other men were frantically offering advice on what to do. Meanwhile, Squirrel left with both of the captain's shoes and then shortly returned to show his own concern for the choking Lum. Suddenly Lum straightened up and showed signs of swallowing.

"It's down. Thank goodness, I got it down," he said in a convincing manner.

"Good," said David, "but you gonna be sick tomorrow. That was a big plug."

Squirrel stepped up to look at his friend, "You sure you are all right?"

The captain, very concerned earlier, now looked at Lum. "Serves you right for chewing so late at night. Now everyone get in bed; reveille at 6:00 a.m."

Lum offered more ham as the three moved back to the tent. Once inside, the three men did everything possible to hold down the laughter. After ten more minutes of whispering about the excited captain, the men drifted off to sleep. It seemed only minutes later that the bugler was announcing reveille.

The three, hardly able to hold back their excitement, got dressed, picked up their muskets, and moved out and in front of their tent, as told to do. David looked back left and then down to the right. Everyone was, 'At Ease,' each in front of his tent. All were waiting for the overzealous captain's appearance. Still he didn't show up. They waited longer.

The captain finally came out of the tent. He was dressed in his well-fitting, gray uniform — except for shoes. He took a couple of steps forward. By then, almost everyone was staring at the officer's sock feet. A snicker was heard, and then another. Then laughter broke out all up and down the line of tents.

They soon realized that the officer was shouting — something about his shoes. The laughter was now even louder than before, as the soldiers realized what had happened.

"Everyone return to your tent immediately," shouted the captain, looking angrily up and down the line of tents. Within ten minutes, the captain, with two soldiers and borrowed shoes, began a search for the captain's shoes.

The first tent searched was that of David, Lum, and Squirrel. Every place in the tent was carefully examined, since they were the prime suspects due to the choking incident the night before. Surprised at not locating the shoes, the searchers moved to the next tent, and so on. Again, the three men had to hold their blankets over their mouths to silence their laughter.

"You throw 'em way out in the weeds?" asked David, looking over at Squirrel.

"No, you 'member that guy Bolton — one from Rover, always buttering up Spook? Called me a runt other day. Well, the shoes are behind his tent."

Lum and David grabbed the blankets and tightened them over their mouths, trying to contain the laughter. Finally, Lum looked over at the serious Squirrel.

"I should've named you rat."

Again, David struggled to hold his laughter. Within half an hour, as everyone was outside his tent awaiting breakfast, a slight commotion was heard near the third tent in row four.

"I didn't do it," someone protested. "Someone planted it; I didn't do it."

And then they heard another, more familiar voice.

"You a real smart aleck," the captain replied.

The three officers soon came by David's tent. One of the officers, a short, chubby man, had Bolton — who continued to protest — by the arm. There were smiles on all of the soldiers' faces as they led the culprit down the row of tents toward the camp's headquarters. Once they had arrived there, they led Bolton, who was still whining, over to a small shed that at one time had served as a tool shed.

"We'll let you know when's time to come out," said the chubby officer as he opened the door. "Now, hush your blabbering."

He closed the door and put the small wooden peg back into the old door hasp. Over the next three days, the captain, though quite angry, was much subdued. Many of the soldiers purposely carried a mock smile when they met him. After day number three, Bolton was released to dig two open latrines for the camp and cover the old ones.

As the three watched Bolton digging the new latrines from a distance, Lum looked at David. "Blue, don't ever get on the wrong side of Squirrel."

"The boy's found his niche in life," Squirrel said about the laboring Bolton, without smiling.

Being around his new friends had caused David to leave his lengthening pity party behind. He was training hard, but he was also having some fun. Within three weeks, the entire camp was talking about what was taking place near Vicksburg, Mississippi. Some Yankee general by the name of Grant — Lum rechristened him Grunt — had the impressive Confederate fort there at Vicksburg under siege. The Federal general had already taken two other Confederate forts on rivers,

Fort Donelson and Fort Henry. Taking Vicksburg, built on a high bluff overlooking the Mississippi River, was not going to be so easy. Grant and an underling by the name of Sherman had already tried to send troops and ironclad gunboats up the Yazoo River north of the strong fortification. That had failed. There were rumors that he was even considering the creation of a canal, by using other nearby rivers, to go around the heavily gunned fort.

By then, Camp Sulphur Springs had about a hundred and twenty-five men training. The men made up the 24th Arkansas Regiment and the 6th Arkansas Artillery Corp. Except for the questionable, new, army food, a cracker-like substance called hardtack, the new soldiers were adjusting quite well to army life.

At the same time, the new trainees at the camp were becoming impressive units, according to the Confederate war officials back in Richmond. At one time, while referring to Captain Spoke, Lum said, "he spoke and the world came into existence." But now, Lum believed that he had a change of heart. No longer was he so high and mighty. He was quite friendly now, and even likable.

"Believe the guy will be a human bean 'fore long. He had better, because we'll turn the Squirrel loose on him," Lum surmised.

In a few days, they received word that the 24th and probably the 6th Artillery unit would be heading for action. No one seemed to know where they might go, but some rumors indicated "down round" Vicksburg. Pemberton's Rebs were still holding out against General Grunt.

As promised, the men were to elect lower ranking officers for the regiment before leaving camp. After a particularly tiresome day of marching and drilling, the near-exhausted men were allowed to take a break and sit down on the side of the hill there in camp. The captain moved in front of the company.

"Men, I want to compliment you on a good month of training. Except for a rotten shoe thief, things have been good," he said and then laughed.

The whole company immediately broke out in laughter. Several turned to look at Sam Bolton, who continued to shake his head no.

"You cheap scudder, you," said Lum, grinning and turning to Squirrel, who had not laughed at the joke.

The captain grew serious as he looked over the men seated in front of him.

"Men, we will be electing two lieutenants, two sergeants, and two corporals. All will be real officers under my command. It is very important that you select leaders — men who will respect rank and the military. We need men who can think under fire — men you can follow into the cave of fear itself. You already know we are not playing games. Many of us will die in this war before it's over. So we need to select those who will give us the best chance to survive and defeat the enemy and bring the war to a close.

The officer election lasted more than an hour, as several men were nominated for each position. David was nominated for sergeant but lost by two votes to a man from Belleville by the name of Jones. After the election, the captain announced the results and recognized the six new officers. The lieutenants were Harvey Bean and Tim Pine, the sergeants were Bill Nigh and Lonnie Howard, and the corporals were Don Hall and Jim Clark. It would remain to be seen what kind of officers the men would be.

Two more days were spent in teaching the new officers their new responsibilities and duties. By the end of the second day, the new lieutenants, Bean and Pine, informed Company I that they would be leaving the next morning. Their destination would be Fort Hindman at Arkansas Post on the Arkansas River. Few of the men had heard of Arkansas Post, let alone Fort Hindman. However, David recalled that his pa had sailed by the post while on his way to Little Rock and wondered if he had stopped there. Lt. Pine — Lum called him Knotty Pine — announced that the group would be leaving the next day for Pine Bluff. From there, assuming the Arkansas River was up, the two military groups would take a paddle wheeler on down to the old Arkansas capital.

Chapter 17

Arkansas Post

September 1862

THE NEXT MORNING, EIGHT wagons with double mule teams were ready. A cavalry unit from Little Rock had also arrived to lead and to trail the military wagon train. Mess wagons were soon ready. After a few words from some unknown colonel, who could not be heard by most of the troops, the wagon train with regimental colors out front began the journey to Pine Bluff.

The early spring continued to be beautiful. The sky was clear and the temperature in the mid-seventies. Even before the wagons left the camp a flock of wild turkey scooted across in front of the cavalry patrol. Pollen was in the air, as attested by several soldiers sneezing. Several farmers, already in the fields, waved as the long, centipede train moved in a southeastern direction.

Lt. Pine had designated David to be the teamster in charge of wagon number four. He had selected Lum and Squirrel as his relief drivers. All three sat in the wagon seat. Twelve other men sat in the wagon behind them on four planks that rested on wooden boxes. Three men were seated together on each plank or seat.

There was much talking and laughter, and even some humorous criticism directed at David when the wagon hit the deeper holes in the rocky road. Each soldier was given enough hardtack for lunch. Since they would not be permitted a lunch break, the men ate the cracker substance as the wagon moved along its route south.

"Blue, you ever think about marrying?" Lum said as he scanned the fields to the left of the wagon train.

"Probably once," David said after a pause, looking back at his companion. "Back in Tennessee, but I wasn't old enough for the little filly."

"Was she good-looking?"

"Well — she was beautiful," David said, looking down at the four mules below them. "Long blonde hair, green eyes, slender. Gosh, what a figure."

"She like you?" Lum asked, seemingly interested.

"Yeah, she sure did, all right," answered David, looking off in the distance to the east again.

"She die?" asked Squirrel, who had been listening to the conversation.

The wagon went over a hole in the road and the riders in the back were roughly jostled about. "Hey, stay out of the gullies up there," someone shouted.

"No, she married a fat preacher, thirty years older than her. Of course, he had a farm, home, and everything," David said, glancing down at the wagon floor.

"I thought she was in love with you instead of the preacher. Should've married you — looks like," replied Lum, looking at David.

"I'd soon as not talk 'bout it."

The other two friends knew it was time to end the conversation. Lum looked over at Squirrel, who was looking at the soldiers in the wagon in front of them.

"You been married before?" Lum joked.

"Eloped once. Only thing, she didn't go with me. Really embarrassing to be standing there at the altar by yourself with jest the preacher — was only one 'I do,'" replied Squirrel without smiling.

Lum and David roared in their laughter about Squirrel's comment. By nightfall, all three boys knew each other even better. Lum turned out to be the oldest of three siblings, and his parents were farmers near Rover. Squirrel was the youngest of six children; all the older ones were girls. His family raised sheep west of Nola. When they discovered that Squirrel had five older sisters, Lum showed some interest.

"Any good-looking ones?"

"Naw, oldest three are married. Glenda, next to me — no you wouldn't want to see her next to me — make two of me. Almost beat me up one time, till I hit her on the head with a frying pan — had grease in it. The other one's got a nose like a moose, red hair, but she's a worker though. Ya'll interested? I'll have you meet 'em."

Both David and Lum were laughing at the way he described his sisters. There was little doubt that these three young men liked each other.

As the moving regiment neared Pine Bluff, David told his companions about his father's murder north of Pine Bluff. Little did David realize that he had just passed the small clearing where his pa had been killed.

The wagons were discarded now, as the soldiers boarded a huge paddle wheeler, with the name on the side, "Memphis Queen." Since none of the men had ridden on a ship before, they were excited to board the ship and experience the ride on down the river. It took a little over an hour to reach Arkansas Post.

The town, founded in 1721 by the French as an important trading post, served as capital of Arkansas territory and later as the first capital of the state in 1836. The site of the original post had changed several times over 140 years due to the changing Mississippi River channel. In 1862, the population of Arkansas Post was around 300. However, an old fort used in the Revolutionary War had been reconstructed. The fort, sitting on a low bluff where the Arkansas River flowed into the Mississippi River, had recently been named Fort Hindman in honor of the rising Arkansas general, Thomas Hindman.

Several large cannon, including eight twelve pounders and several six pounders, along with a couple of James Rifles, were positioned in the fort, with the hope of controlling any enemy river traffic coming off the adjacent Mississippi River. With Union General Grant's recent victories over Fort Donelson and Fort Henry, and now his siege of the Vicksburg fortress, the Federals hoped to soon control the entire Mississippi River and divide the Confederacy. Governor Rector and the Arkansas War Board had earlier approved of the revamped fort, in the hope of keeping Federal ships from moving up the Arkansas River and destroying the Delta area, the breadbasket of Arkansas.

As the Memphis Queen moved into dock at Arkansas Post, every soldier aboard was at the ship's railing trying to see the town and the often-mentioned Fort Hindman. For most of the Arkansas men, the town was a disappointment, but from a distance the fort looked impressive. As the men disembarked, Lum looked over to the dock area.

"Where's the band and the young women?"

"Don't know, but if I had womenfolk, I would remove them from this place. Gonna be fighting here someday," answered David, scanning the area.

"Fort looks strong, though," Squirrel added.

Chapter 18

Fort Hindman

January 1863

SERIOUS TRAINING OF A different kind got underway almost immediately. Patrols were established up and down the Arkansas River, on both sides of the river. Patrols were assigned along the west bank of the Mississippi River in case enemy troops were dropped off there in preparation for a siege of the fort. Sentries were placed at strategic locations over a mile from the fort, on the west side of the Mississippi River, and on the north side of the Arkansas River. A series of lookout points were established in order to scan up river and down river. These outposts were in touch at all times during the day with flag codes. Even at night, code messages were sent by use of lantern codes. Surveillance was good, and every effort was made to examine any suspicious move that might be signs of the enemy's presence along either of the large rivers.

With Grant's control of the upper Mississippi River, Arkansas state government officials were also quite worried about a Union effort to gain control of the lower Arkansas River and even threaten Little Rock upstream. While Grant had his hands full with his failed efforts at taking Vicksburg, everyone knew that he would probably take it if given enough time and enough men.

With careful surveillance along the Mississippi River, the Reb army continued the patrols and training exercises. There was also a lot of hard labor as the defenses of the fort were strengthened. More than 500 bales of cotton were brought into the fort to be used as cover in case the fort was shelled from the outside. Shell and gunpowder were covered. Training exercises included, on signal, men rushing to their assigned posts. The 8th Arkansas Artillery Corps continued for hours a day simulating aiming, loading, and firing procedures.

Troops continued to arrive at Fort Hindman over the next five months. According to one man that David had overheard, more than 4,000 Rebs were now part of the defense team for Fort Hindman and Arkansas Post. Most of the soldiers were put to work digging rifle pits anywhere from a quarter of a mile to two miles north of the fort. The idea was to slow any invaders coming overland.

January, as usual, was very cold in Arkansas. Yet, Brigadier General Thomas Churchill was determined to hold the gateway to the Arkansas River. The Yell County trio had worked for days in the near freezing weather digging in the embankments of the heights around the fort. David and Lum swung the fifteen-pound pickaxes, while Squirrel scooped up the clodded soil and rock and tossed it down in front of the rifle pits. Bales of cotton would be added later for the men to stay behind.

"Blooming ground is frozen; can't get any deeper than two inches," complained Lum.

"My hands are frozen; let's go over to the fire," said David, looking over at Squirrel, who had just thrown another shovelful of soil outside the forming rifle pit. The threesome climbed out of the pit and moved over to the fire that had been built for warming the soldier's hands. Two men from Company I were standing there very close to the fire.

"It's my toes; I can't even feel 'em," the short, stocky soldier said. "You'uns not cold, are ya?" the man asked, looking down at the flames.

"How many ya'll dug?" asked Squirrel, referring to the number of rifle pits.

"Second one today. Done better 'cept fer the rocks; 'bout ever third shovel hits bedrock," the heavier man replied.

"You guys see that ironclad paddle wheeler go by on the Mississippi while 'go? We's on the lower level, and we could barely see it through the trees. Had U.S. flag, so it was Union," the first man added.

"No, didn't see it," answered David.

Captain Spoke had walked up to the fire after examining the partially dug pits. "Good job, men. Think we got about thirty or so ready here on Coines Hill — 'nother forty or so down lower." The captain looked over at the first two men. "You men also from Texas?"

"Yeah, dismounted cavalry — though rather be on a horse someplace else," answered the stocky soldier.

"I bet we have 4,000 men from Texas here already — close to a 1,000 Arkys," offered Spoke.

"See you men," the officer said, moving on down the hillside. In the distance, the bugle was sounding. It was suppertime.

"What is the date," Lum asked, as the three Arkys started back to the fort area.

"January 8," answered Squirrel.

"Hmmm, that's Ma's birthday. Bet they will celebrate back home in Bluffton tonight," David said. Sure wish I were there around that big fireplace eating some of ma's pork chops, he thought. Then he thought, January 10 was Lillie's birthday. He wondered if she had any children yet.

It was announced after supper that a chapel meeting would be held that evening at 7:00 p.m. in the fort chapel. All were invited to attend and hear one of the army chaplains talk.

"You guys going?" asked Lum.

"Yow," replied Squirrel.

David said nothing.

"Hey, Blue, you going tonight?"

"Doubt it. You guys can go," he said, looking away.

"You not one of them atheists, are you?" Lum said in a joking manner.

David didn't reply. Later, as Lum and Squirrel started to leave for the chapel service, Lum again asked David to go with them.

"All right; need som'in to do," David replied.

The speaker, an artilleryman from Little Rock, was about thirty years of age.

"Men, we will probably see serious battle in a few days. Been some heavy traffic on the Mississippi River last three or four days. The question is not whether we live or die in battle, but instead, are we ready to meet our maker? Many will die, but how many will live again someday in heaven? The most important thing we can do is not to be ready for the Yanks, but to be ready to meet the Lord. My own brother died at the fall of Fort Donelson — killed by a sharpshooter. My greatest fear is, was he ready to go? Ever since, I have become a stronger believer. Men, God loves you. He cares for you. He will protect you from all harm. But, we must put our trust in Jesus Christ."

Lum and Squirrel were listening intently to the chaplain. David was picking at the sole of his shoe. He thought, I've heard this before. He sure took care of my pa, who was a strong believer. Took care of the parson back in Tennessee by allowing him to have my girlfriend. Shor does take care them slaves at the auction. Probably ready to pass the collection plate now — that's the part they really like. By then the chaplain was finishing.

"Let's all sing, 'Love is Supreme,' on page 31."

Although they had no music, the men sang loudly on all three verses. David stood reverently, but only looked down at his hands on the back of the chair in front of him. The service ended, but most of the men stayed in the chapel to visit for a while, since it was much warmer in the chapel than in the unheated tents on the outside.

Lum looked at his two friends.

"He'll make you think," he said, referring to the chaplain. "Course, I've been in church my whole life — always been a believer."

"Me too. My pa taught my Sunday school class when I was about twelve," Squirrel said, looking at David.

"You probably raised in church too, I'll bet, Blue?" asked Lum, looking over at David.

"Yeah, I was," he said.

~~~

David found it difficult to go to sleep that night. Long after the other two men were breathing heavy in sleep, he lay there thinking. Was there a God who observed and interfered in the lives of mankind?

It seemed like he had hardly turned over before he heard the bugle. It can't be six o'clock, he thought, as the other two men stirred. Both Lum and Squirrel sat up. Lum reached for the pocket watch that his parents had given him as a going away gift. The bugler blew the horn again — this time the alert signal.

"It's only 3:00 a.m.," Lum said, looking at the watch.

Again, the alert signal sounded.

"Hurry. We got to get to our station," reminded Squirrel.

After dressing, the men quickly exited the tent to see men running in all directions.

"Battle stations! Battle stations!" screamed Captain Spoke.

Most of the men had their haversacks and their muskets. Most were either jogging or running. Unfortunately, men were running in both directions, frequently running into each other. As the three rounded the outside, west corner of the fort, Lum speculated that it was probably a drill — a drill to emphasize preparedness. David wasn't sure about that — it looked like the real thing.

Up ahead, several officers were telling men to occupy the lower rifle pits first. A munitions wagon, pulled by mules, was already there. As the men jogged on around the outside of the fort, they could hear officers inside the fort screaming orders. By the time David and the other two had reached the northwest corner of the fort, other soldiers were waiting to move down into the gun pits on the hillside. David thought, what would it be like if it wasn't a clear night?

One of the lieutenants, Bill Nigh, was directing soldiers to the different level gun pits.

"Take number three, there," said the officer, pushing David and looked on back to the waiting men.

The three friends dropped down in the pit. The pit was about chest deep, except for Squirrel. His head was just above the level of the embankment mound in front of the pit. Men were still running by to get to the empty gun pits.

Off in the distance, a bugler sounded advance. Almost 2,000

Confederate soldiers were ready to march toward the north, where there was apparently a Union threat. Other soldiers were bringing shell and powder in the form of cartridges. Each soldier was given forty rounds of ammo.

"We'll bring more later," stated a young sergeant.

By then, it was either getting lighter or the men's eyes were adjusting to the night. David could barely see another 400 to 500 Reb soldiers marching in a northeastern direction. He also knew that rifle pits were as far away as two miles.

Evidently, the Union troops had been transported through the White River cutoff and were going to begin an assault north of the fort. David looked up to see a rider hurrying from the north. Another officer, Colonel James Dreshler, quickly met him. David could hear the messenger, trying to yell over all the noise.

"They are ashore at Nortrebe's Plantation, sir," the man yelled.

"Ride to Colonel Dunningham's headquarters," the colonel screamed at an aide. "Tell him Federals ashore at Nortrebe's Plantation. Might want to check with sentries on the south side of the river as well — and hurry."

David noticed a unit of cavalry riding north with a trailing small cannon.

The sun would soon be above the trees in the distance. It would be light enough to see. Then, from the north, the men could hear small cannon fire, and then rifle fire. David realized that the battle had begun. They soon heard gunfire on the south side of the river. The enemy was there as well.

"Look," Squirrel yelled, pointing out toward the river. "Ships — Yankee ships."

There were three ships, although they did not seem to be approaching. They were possibly the transport ships that had dropped off Union infantry, both on the north and the south side of the Arkansas River. Within a short time, the ships were out of sight.

Chapter 19

Defeat

THE DAY DRUG ON as sporadic gunfire continued on both sides of the Arkansas River. Little did the 5,000 Rebs realize that that they were now facing only a part of the 33,000-man Union operation. Later in the morning, troops occupying the trenches and rifle pits began to realize that the Rebs, stationed a mile or so out from the fort, were slowly retreating back toward the fort. As yet, the big guns of the fort had not been fired.

By 2:00 p.m., most of the Rebs had pulled back closer to Fort Hindman. Hospital wagons had continued to move back and forth from the area north of the fort. However, the retreating Rebs in the distance were also taking many Union lives. Around 4:00 p.m., soldiers in the fort could see several ships of different sizes east on the river. Soon, observers could clearly see four or five Union ironclads move out of the huge Union flotilla and strike toward the fort. David, Lum, and Squirrel watched the ironclads draw near, knowing that they would bring a devastating fire on and around the fort.

"It's going to be bad," Squirrel said, looking out to the moving ironclads.

"They can't get too much closer or they will hit the huge log jam we put down along the riverbank," David said as they nervously waited.

At 400 yards or so, the boats opened a furious cannonade. One of the first ships, the USS Rattler, crashed against the log piles and was torn apart. They could see several members of the Union navy in the water, trying to swim and survive.

The other three ironclads continued their fire. The heavy, naval shells ranged in size from thirty to 105 pounds. Inside the fort, the field cannon grew hot from the continued use, as the Rebs tried to stop the unmerciful cannonade. Slowly, the walls of the fort were breaking, crumbling, and falling. As the shelling intensified, the men outside the fort in the rifle pits stayed down in the bottom of the pits. Several shells hit the trenches, killing several men at one time, as the terrible cannon fire continued from the gunboats until dark.

It was not until dark that the Rebs were able to assess the damages both inside and outside the fort. At best count, more than sixty Rebs had died either inside or outside the fort. The men under siege could do little to strengthen the damaged fort.

Around 7:00 p.m., David, Lum, and Squirrel were able to eat an evening meal of hardtack and water. All three had to go to the latrine, although they had to urinate in the gun pit during the day's shelling. The men were exhausted from the hellish afternoon. As they sat in the pit, they talked about the terrible day that they had experienced.

"I thought the Yanks would never quit firing. I can't believe that they could reload those mortars and Rodmans as fast as they did. Those Union guys that carried shell all day are bound to be tired," David said, looking up at the darkened sky.

"From watching our medical corps over the last hour or so, we must have had hundreds killed along this hillside or inside the fort," added Lum.

"I'd rather be here than inside the fort. They's a lot of dead men in there, I bet," Squirrel said as he looked back to the damaged walls of the fort.

"Course, the Feds took it bad, too. That one gunboat just fell apart on getting hit by our cannon and then smashing against the big log pile," observed David. "Never heard of being shelled for two hours and never even being able to shoot your musket. Course, there were no Fed infantry in our area; they would'a been killed by their own navy."

Just then a medical corpsman approached the gun pit.

"Any injuries or deaths here?" the man asked.

"No, but I peed my pants," replied Lum.

"Ya'll are lucky then. Lot of men killed outside here in the trenches — really bad inside too," the corpsman said as he moved on down the line of rifle pits.

"Hey, we supposed to stay here?" Lum hollered at the corpsman.

"Reckon so — far as I know," he replied without looking back.

"Bet the Fed infantry will come tomorrow — 'specially with the holes in the walls of the fort," speculated Lum. "Just softened us up today."

"You know, my ears are still ringing from the cannon noise. Never heard anything so loud in my life," observed Squirrel.

"Men," asked Lum, "reckon we should have a short prayer?"

"Yeah, go ahead, Lum," replied Squirrel. David said nothing.

"Lord, we's alive here in the pit. They's dead all 'round us; course, reckon you are able to see us. The corpsman said we was really lucky — may have been more than that. We feel that your Almighty hand may have been over our rifle pit. We're saying thank you for caring for us. Amen. Oh, Lord, forgot — be with the families of those killed here today — on both sides. Now amen."

As Lum looked up, he noticed that David had not bowed

his head during the prayer. He was staring out in the direction of the river, deep in thought.

There was no way to get comfortable in the rifle pit, but the three men were able to get a few hours of sleep. Near sunrise, an unknown officer came by the pit.

"Men, the Feds are advancing from the north, again. Our men in that area are falling back. You will see Union infantry before long. Ammo supply all right?"

"Didn't fire a shell yesterday. Nothing to shoot at, 'cept ships, and they are too fur away," David said, glancing back north.

After a visit to the latrine and some much-needed walking to relieve their cramped leg muscles, the three stood above the pit and looked out on the river. The water slowly moved south to eventually become part of the larger Mississippi River. A flock of snow geese flew overhead, most likely looking about for a good grain field. A dog was barking someplace in the town of Arkansas Post.

"Except for the battered fort, you wouldn't know war was going on," observed David, scanning the area west of the fort.

"Even wonder why we fightin'? Life is so short, yet we make it shorter. Our politicians decide the right thing and young men divide up and butcher each other," Lum observed in an unusually serious moment.

"Yeah, imagine what we would be doing today if not for this stupid war?" questioned Squirrel.

"I'd be courting that ugly sister of yours," Lum joked as he looked over at Squirrel and smiled.

Suddenly, they could hear rifle fire back north again. Then they heard a bugle. The loud blasts of cannon fire followed. David looked back to his left, where several Reb soldiers were forming rank. Within fifteen minutes, the group, probably more than 800 men, had begun to march north toward the sound of battle.

Still, no cannon fire reached this area 100 yards north of the fort. Soon, Confederate cannon, on the outside of the fort, began to answer the Union artillery greetings. A couple of couriers rode by on horses in the general direction of the apparent battle. A couple of supply wagons, along with a mule-pulled ambulance, were now headed north.

David noticed that most of the Rebs in the rifle pits had gotten out of their pits and were also anxiously looking back north. Then a galloping cavalry patrol moved in a northwest direction. Suddenly, they heard loud cannon blasts from the south across the river, followed by sporadic rifle fire. As the three men glanced back to the south, they noticed a lot of activity around the top of the damaged fort. The activity across the Arkansas River had gotten the attention of General Churchill and his staff.

"Yanks coming both directions. Course, those on south side will have to cross the river," analyzed Squirrel. "Wonder if they will drop off any more troops closer to the fort?"

"Hey, let's eat some steak and taters," joked Lum as he pulled out some hardtack.

Several other men on the slope were also eating their least favorite meal. They seemed to realize that they must eat before the activity got closer. David took a long drink from the canteen, and suddenly jerked it away from his mouth.

"Look! Ships!" he said as he looked east down river.

All three men were looking in the direction of the ships when another bugle sounded.

"Didn't the people in the fort see they were approaching?" asked Lum, looking at David.

"They asleep up there?"

As the men watched, they soon realized that there were several ships. In front, leading the convoy, were the aggressive ironclads. Officers were now all over the slopes leading up to Fort Hindman. Commands were being shouted to the men in the rifle pits. By then, Captain Spoke had reached David's rifle pit.

"Men, we are probably going to be shelled again. Stay down, but occasionally check out the area around the water. They might drop troops here as well."

Spoke quickly moved down to the other rifle pits. By then the activity back north had really increased, as the two armies exchanged cannon fire. Across the river to the south, gunfire increased. The Yankee advance was well coordinated.

The men had dropped down in the rifle pits and were waiting for the attack. Lord help us, thought David, and then he remembered that he had just about given up on this God, who seemed to be blessing the Yankees at the present time. Maybe he had listened to their prayers. He raised his head slightly above the rim of the pit and looked down the river. He could see at least parts of the seven ships behind the approaching ironclads.

"They are getting in range —" Before he finished his comment, cannon up in the fort fired. David could see big splashes made in the water by the fort's cannonballs. The ironclads were almost in range.

"Men, we're gonna catch it again," David said, slumping down with his back to the front of the deep hole.

The ironclad navy then released a terrible, simultaneous blast. The sound was almost deafening. While the fort's field guns responded, other sounds were created, as parts of the damaged fort began to fall, forward and backward. Even with the terrible mortars and cannon fire, the three friends could hear screams of injured men.

The three men sat on the ground at the bottom of the four-foot deep gun pit, looking above at the sky, as if expecting a shell to hit at any time. David looked over at Lum, who seemed to be praying silently. Pray hard, David thought. He glanced back to the other end of the pit and up above. Men were on the ground level, running.

"What's going on?" David said aloud.

Then a huge shell hit just above but outside of the pit — and then another shell a little further away. The men heard screaming.

"Believe a shell hit in the next pit over — that's Hall, Nowlin, and Clark," yelled Lum.

David stared above at the open sky. Dust, smoke, and debris flew through the air. A man from above suddenly came sliding down into the pit, landing on Squirrel. He immediately scrambled to his feet, reached for the rim of the rifle pit, put his right foot on Squirrel, and leaped up to the ground level, where he landed on his stomach.

"Run! Run! Get away!" he screamed as he scrambled to his feet.

David, sitting at the bottom of the pit now watching the frightened soldier, saw him as he quickly got to his feet. In a split second, the man literally exploded when a large shell hit him in the middle of the back. His head and arms became projectiles. Almost at the same time, an object hit David across the face. He thought shrapnel had hit him. Reaching for his face, he found blood, but then he realized that it wasn't his. One of the arms of the man who had been hit by a shell had struck him from above; the blood belonged to him.

Then a huge cannon ball hit the back of the pit, not over eight inches above Squirrel's head. The shell buried at least three feet into the embankment. David, hearing the heavy impact, quickly raised his head to see if the other two men were all right.

Squirrel had pulled his knees up to his stomach and sat there with his arms around them in a compact manner. He was looking around in a crazed manner as tears moved down his dirty face. David thought that if he or Lum had been sitting there instead of Squirrel, their heads would have been blown off. Lum, pray again or something!

The afternoon proved to be an evening from hell itself as the Federal guns blasted the fort in Arkansas Post for three long hours. At almost 4:00 p.m., the Federal navy guns began to slack off and soon stopped altogether. The fort's big guns had already been silenced for almost an hour. Yet in the distance, the men in the rifle pit could hear much gunfire — now mostly musket fire.

Bugles were sounded two or three times. The combined burned powder and dust in the air had created a hazy, cloudy afternoon. None of the three had spoken for a while. Now, with the decreasing bombardment, Lum looked at both of his friends.

"Not over," he said. "When the naval guns quit firing, they are allowing their infantry to move in for the kill. Let's get ready to fight."

As David looked over the rim of the pit, he could see Union soldiers, moving in a disciplined line, advancing from the north. He saw thousands of men. There seemed to be little resistance to the Union advance now.

The Rebs in the gun pits turned from facing the river, back towards the impressive line of men in blue. The Southerners soon began to fire at the oncoming Federals, but it became more difficult, since the Federals were beginning to use small, cavalry drawn cannon on the Rebs.

Chapter 20

Prisoners of War

January 1863

THE FIGHT WENT ON for another half hour. Squirrel slowly raised his head above the pit to prepare to fire his musket.

"They's a white flag — and another one. Our men are getting out of the trenches. They are surrendering. Our officers are surrendering."

By then, both David and Lum were up watching the developments taking place about a hundred yards away. However, another Reb officer ran up to where the first white flag of surrender was raised and began to argue with the officer that had surrendered. Momentarily a second officer ran up to also protest.

But most of the Rebs had already laid down their guns. It was too late for the Rebs to back out of surrender. The men still in the rifle pits and ditches slowly crawled out of the fortifications and laid their guns on the ground. Federal soldiers were already coming around to collect the Reb's muskets.

As the trio watched the proceedings, they noticed four or five Confederate staff officers coming from the damaged fort. General Churchill, the commander of the fort, was in the group. David and the other two began to walk down to where the Reb's surrender had occurred. As they got closer, they saw Churchill go over to the officer that had initiated the surrender. His language was pointed and plain.

"Who gave you the authority to surrender, might I ask?"

"A member of your own staff asked me to surrender," protested the officer, Colonel John Garland, as another officer arrived.

"We have not surrendered at all, and we will continue to fight," said Colonel James Deshler, who commanded the Confederate right flank. He changed his mind, however, when General Sherman, one of the Federal generals standing there, reminded him that most of his men had already been disarmed.

By the end of the day, 4,700 Confederates had surrendered. They had fought well, inflicting more than 1,000 casualties while suffering approximately 140 casualties, yet almost an entire Confederate army had been captured.

The Confederates were rounded up and moved to a field northwest of the demolished fort. Several hundred Federal soldiers, as guards, surrounded the Rebel prisoners, who were now standing or sitting on the cold ground. As the men sat waiting on their eventual fate, David, Lum, and Squirrel talked about the two-day battle.

"We don't got a navy, and shooting at the fort was like shootin' pigeons in the barrel. Course, they had lot more infantry," Lum said, looking around at the other prisoners.

"Know what I heard a Yankee say? Said they had 32,000 men and we had, what, 4,000?" David surmised.

"What was that going on 'bout the surrender, anyway?" asked Squirrel, looking back at David.

"Apparently, Churchill and other officers did not want to surrender — sounds like a mistake or something," added David.

"Reckon what they going to do with us?" Squirrel asked again. "Think they will let us go?"

Other Confederates nearby overheard the conversation. A clean-cut, Confederate lieutenant moved over to the Yell County men.

"Lee's taking prisoners back East — imagine we will go to a prison camp some place. We know the Yanks have several camps back North," the Reb officer offered.

In about two hours, the Federal army moved several mess wagons into the large, captive circle. As the men waited in line to reach one of the wagons, several Union officers came into the captive area and asked all of the Confederate officers to report to the fort's gate.

"Bet it's hardtack," Lum said as he looked over men in front of him toward the mess wagon. The men were shocked when the Union cooks dipped out brown beans and ham hock.

"Hey, let's join the Fed army," exclaimed Lum. "They know how to feed."

After the meal, the prisoners were moved inside the half-demolished fort for the night. Fires were built, and for the most part, the Confederates slept reasonably well. They had a decent breakfast the next morning, and then the Union guards selected a Confederate burial detail to bury the sixty Rebs that had been killed. The eighty wounded Confederates also received reasonable care. A Union burial detail buried the 134 Federal soldiers that had died. It was a greater problem to provide for the 898 wounded Union soldiers.

David was one of the Rebs selected to help bury the Confederates that had died. He and the other members of the burial detail were aghast at the condition of some of the dead soldiers. Several members of the burial detail became ill after viewing some of their fellow comrades. Some of the men had lost legs or arms. One man's upper torso was found. One man had been decapitated.

David thought about the day before, when the Reb had fallen into their gun pit. Would anyone ever know that he had been killed? There was little talking as the Rebs buried their fellow soldiers. As David shoveled dirt and carried the dead, he thought about life in general. Why would a God allow such a massacre — such horror? Who did God bless this time? After all, the winners, the Feds, had far more casualties than the losers. How could people believe in such nonsense? After all, both the Federals and the Confederates believed in the same God. It was the same God that the poor slaves on the plantation believed in when they sang to him at the brush arbor.

By 11:00 a.m., the Federal staff had told the prisoners where they would be going. The commanding Union general, McClernard, was not at the battle site. He had made arrangements for the captured prisoners to be sent on to Springfield, Illinois. Some would be put into the prison camp there at Camp Butler, while others would go on to still another camp that the Rebs had never heard of, Camp Douglas in Chicago.

While inside the fort eating the meal prepared by the Union soldiers, the Rebs had not noticed three large, steam-powered paddle wheelers move up river to the Arkansas Post wharf. As they ate, David, Lum, and Squirrel talked about the voyage north to Illinois.

"Reckon any chance to escape?" Lum asked as he looked around at the guards. "You guys swim good?"

"I can hardly swim — dog paddle little," Squirrel replied, looking over at Lum.

Thinking back to saving his sister's life, David glanced over at Lum. "I can swim okay."

"You'uns not aiming to abandon ship on me, are ya?" Squirrel questioned, with a worried look on his face.

"Naw, we going to need you, Squirrel — way you can climb," Lum said, glancing back to the gate of the fort.

The Union guards were now taking forty to fifty men at a time out the fort gate.

"They taking us someplace," David said.

In about a half hour, the blue-clad guards came over near Company I. One of the guards, a slightly built man with a handlebar mustache, walked up behind David and roughly touched him with the soldier's bayonet.

"Up, Johnnies."

David leaped to his feet and whirled around, facing the man with the musket/bayonet.

"Yank, you hit me with that bayonet again and I will take it away from you and saw off that stupid mustache."

The surprised guard took a step back as Lum roared out with laughter.

"Bet he's never seen a battle. Probably guards the latrine all day," Lum said, referring to the guard.

The guard said nothing more as the three men slowly got to their feet. A line of Confederate soldiers had formed in front of them, so the three Rebs got at the end of it.

"Blue, you scared General Grunt to death back there," Lum said as he looked over at David and laughed.

"You don't reckon we ought to turn Squirrel loose on him?"

"I'll keep my eyes on him," Squirrel replied, "and give it some serious thinking."

David thought back to Squirrel's placing the captain's shoes behind the tent of the man that had called him a runt. As the Rebs moved west toward the town of Arkansas Post, they noticed the three paddle wheelers docked at the wharf. The long line of Rebs soon reached the first paddle wheeler, USS Comstock. The men slowly filed onto the ship. The ship, with iron plating on the sides, was well armed; several heavy, naval guns were placed in key positions. The ship, powered by steam, had two tall smokestacks. The steamer had three levels.

Reb prisoners kept coming on board even after it seemed to be full of men. David reasoned, if three ships could carry the 4,700 men, then each ship had to carry around 1,500 men. Even after the first ship was loaded, it took almost three hours to load the last two.

As David watched the last ship being loaded, he noticed that several wounded Rebs were put on it. Some of the wounded men were on crutches, while others were carried on board on stretchers. It was around 6:00 p.m. before the ship's loud whistles blew and the shore men released the heavy cables holding the big war ships to the wharf.

By midnight, the ships were passing Memphis. David watched as the ship slowly moved by the river port without a stop. He remembered the city where he had observed the slave auction with his pa and brothers. He thought about his pa seeing the rest of the family off on the ferry before he took his ill-fated trip down river and on to Pine Bluff. He really missed his pa, but he also missed his ma and the rest of the family. Would he ever see them again?

David watched the city of Memphis, as the ships slowly moved north toward their destination.

"Ever been in Memphis?" asked a stranger who had walked up beside him. The soldier was also looking toward the city.

After a pause, David looked at the soldier.

"Yeah, use to live in Hickory Flats."

"Really? I've been there, time or two," the man answered in a surprised tone. "Got a cousin who used to live in Memphis —

big Reb general now. You probably heared of him — General Nathan Bedford Forrest."

"Yeah, General Forrest," David said, looking back at the man. "He's given the Yanks — Hey, wait. Did he own a slave auction there in Memphis?"

"Sur did. I worked there a year or so. Wish I had been there when the war started; I'd be in his cavalry now, 'stead of going to a prisoner camp. Ya know, Nathan sold slaves and used slaves on his plantation, yet he has freed slaves riding in his cavalry unit."

David had been listening carefully to the man.

"David Lofland," he said, reaching out his hand toward the man. "Live in Bluffton, Arkansas now."

"Earl Forrest," the soldier said, quickly extending his hand toward David. "Helena, Arkansas. Good to meet you, David."

"Married, Earl?" asked David.

"Yeah, and one child — little girl."

"Well, Earl, we might as well become friends. We going to be living in the same place," David said.

"You bet. Guess we better hit the sack. See you tomorrow, David," Earl said as he walked away.

David stood there a while after Earl left, staring at the water. He wondered how Lillie was doing in Hickory Flats. He would still like to see her someday.

Two days later, the three ships arrived at St. Louis. Except for taking on a supply of coal for the steam engines, they spent little time in the huge city. The steamers moved on north of St. Louis and then turned north up the Illinois River.

By then, the Reb prisoners were growing restless. A serious fight broke out two days after the ship left St. Louis. A Union soldier pushed a Reb in order to get around him. The Reb quickly turned and pushed the guard, causing him to fall backwards. Within seconds, the inflamed Reb was on top of the guard, and he managed to get the guard's rifle across his throat. The commotion caused other guards to quickly move to the area and see what was going on. For a minute or two the Rebs, who had circled the scuffle, prevented the Union guards from getting to the fight. In the meantime, the angry Reb sitting on top of the guard was able to get up and disappear among the prisoners at the other end of the ship.

For some reason, none of the Confederates watching the encounter could remember who the guilty Reb was or even what he looked like. As the embarrassed guard started to get up from the deck of the ship, Lum stepped forward and reached out his hand to him.

"Here — don't want to mess with Rebs, 'lessen you have them heavily outnumbered." The guard jerked his hand back as the watching Rebs roared in laughter.

The ships moved north one more day before coming to Beardstown, a small town on the Illinois River. The first ship stopped and 500 to 600 prisoners were dropped off. These Rebs would eventually board wagons and be taken about sixty miles east to Springfield. David heard one of the Union soldiers refer to Camp Butler, the prisoner of war camp at the capital of Illinois.

"Be bad to spend time in a prison in Lincoln's hometown," Earl said. He had now begun spending most of his time with David.

"Guess it's Chicago for us then," Squirrel said as the two loaded ships proceeded up river. "Never believed I'd ever see Illinois."

Two days later, after the ships had passed Peoria, another serious incident occurred onboard the ship. It was late morning, as David and Squirrel walked along on the lower deck, when they saw a prisoner suddenly climb up on the ship's railing and then leap out into the murky waters of the river. Guards immediately ran to the scene. One of them quickly raised his musket and aimed toward the swimming escapee. Squirrel, close by, threw himself at the guard, hitting him as he pulled the trigger.

"Who pushed me?" screamed Squirrel. "I'm tired of you guys bullying me." He slowly got up off the deck, turned to the guard, and said, "Sorry. Need to shoot the guy who pushed me."

Unfortunately, one of the other guards had shot the escaping Reb. It was not a serious wound, but it slowed the now struggling swimmer. A second guard glanced at an officer who had been watching the prisoner.

"Gonna stop and get him?"

"No, let him drown — be a good lesson for the Johnnies," the officer said as he smiled at the Rebs near the ship's railing and walked away.

Chapter 21

Chicago

THE THIRD DAY, THE steamships made it to the southern part of Chicago where they were docked. From the ship's dock, the prisoners were moved to a waiting train for a short ride to the Chicago train station. After reaching the station, they were made to walk to the Chicago prisoner of war camp.

The newspapers had evidently carried stories for days about the battle for Fort Hindman, the captured prisoners, and the prisoner assignment to the camp in Chicago, because curious onlookers who wanted to see the traitors from the South lined the streets. As the men trudged down the street, the Chicago residents made many comments about the dirty arrivals.

"They don't even have uniforms," someone said.

"Awful dirty looking," a lady observed. "Look like criminals.

"So these are the slaveholders — they look worse than slaves — certainly dirtier," a well-dressed man observed.

"Feel sorry for them," said a grandmotherly looking lady. "They look hungry to me."

"Hope they are closely guarded," David heard a Chicago policeman say.

As they walked on toward the camp, two young boys were standing near a light pole on the street corner. They were staring at what must have been an unbelievable sight. When Lum got up close to where the boys were, he turned toward them.

"Boo," he said, taking a step in their direction.

The boys quickly ran back toward the crowd.

"Feds ought to pay us for the sideshow," said Earl, looking at Squirrel. "We are the attraction of the day."

By then, the Rebs in the front of the moving column could see their new home. There was a huge gate and above was an impressive sign, "Camp Douglas."

"Home, sweet home," observed Lum. "Bet the food is good here."

One of the first things that David noticed was the compound fence. It was only about six feet high, which seemed odd for a prison enclosure. As the men approached the gate, David noticed several nice buildings, maybe a block south of the prison facility. As he glanced back toward the brick buildings, he surmised that the impressive buildings must be a hospital or important government buildings. Then he saw another sign, University of Chicago.

"Hey, Lum, they's got a college here,," David said, smiling. "We gonna git educated here in Chicago."

"Believe me, Blue, we gonna git educated while we are here, but not the way you talking about," responded Lum, looking at the impressive-looking buildings.

The long lines of prisoners had stopped moving up near the gate of the camp. The wind was blowing harder now. Seeing Chicago and the curious crowds of people watching them had caused the men to forget about the icy temperatures of late January.

"Gosh, never this cold in Arkansas," commented Squirrel, standing with his arms folded and shaking. A nearby guard overheard the comment.

"Hey Reb, this is warm. Wait a week or so, be down 10°

below zero. When that north wind really blows across Lake Michigan, you'll have icicles on your noses," he laughed.

After another half hour or so, the freezing prisoners discovered why there was a delay. They were entering the camp according to the company and regiment to which they belonged. A Reb officer, probably a Reb adjutant, was checking off the men according to their company. The Federals were going to have the correct names and the number of prisoners in each company.

After a time, a Federal soldier called out Regiment 24, Company I. Confederate soldiers in front began to step aside to allow the members of Company I to move to the front of the line. The adjutant of Company I, Oney Taylor, was standing near the gate with a Union officer covered with gold braid. After a brief delay, six members of I Company were checked off. All money and valuables were taken from the men and recorded on a roster. Then the Rebs passed under the huge sign, Camp Douglas, and on into the facility.

Chapter 22

Camp Douglas

SURPRISINGLY, THE CAMP APPEARED to be quite impressive. There were at least 300 or more acres in the facility. The camp had been divided up into four parts. One section included the post headquarters, the officer headquarters, the post office, and a parade ground. A different section of the camp had the prison hospital and morgue. At the far end of the camp was a stable area. On the western side of the camp was a series of long barracks, 105 feet long and 24 feet wide, all built on blocks. The buildings set up off the ground almost two feet. Looking at the layout, David reasoned that there must be forty or fifty of the long barracks. He noticed that tar paper covered the roofs.

As the seven men from Company I stood waiting, another Union officer soon arrived to speak with adjutant Taylor.

"You men will be housed in barrack number 87. You will be with the 8th Mississippi Regiment, captured at Fort Donelson, and a couple of other Arkansas companies. Be 180 men in the barrack. Follow me."

"You hear that Lum — 180 men in our building," David commented, as they continued to look around and follow the Union officer. "How many men they got here?"

Within five minutes, the men arrived at barrack 87. They wondered why none of the prisoners were outside. Then, David thought, why would they be outside in this freezing weather?

The adjutant checked off the men's names on a list and handed it to the Union officer.

"All right, let's go inside," the officer stated in a bored manner.

The seven men stepped inside the long building. Already, there was a smell — of dirty clothes and unwashed bodies. There were two rows of double bunk beds, one row against the left wall, and a second row against the right wall. In between was an aisle about nine feet wide.

As David glanced around at their new home, he noticed that there was no ceiling, only rafters and braces extending across the width of the building. The outside walls were of single thickness pine board. There appeared to be a large wood stove down toward the far end of the building.

"We got rules and you better learn them as soon as possible or pay the consequences," David heard the Union officer say. "First, no lights — that being candles — after 10:00 p.m. The privy is out back of the barracks. But, after 9:00 p.m., you will use one of the slop jars. Anyone outside of the barrack after 9:00 p.m. will be considered an escaping prisoner and will be shot. You will learn to plan for your privy trips. Also, we have what we call a dead line — a space of ten feet near the camp fences. You get in that space and you will get a mini ball in the head. I'd stay fifteen feet away from the fence. There are guard towers ever so often, and we can see everything going on inside the camp.

"Every Reb who comes in here starts thinking about escape. I won't tell you how many Rebs have been shot trying to escape. Behave yourself and you may survive until your army surrenders. You can git more information from the Mississippi men down there," the guard said, nodding toward the men at the end of the barrack. "That is if you can understand them. All you Southerds talk in a queer way, anyway."

The officer turned around and left the barrack. David looked down at the end of the barrack where the men continued to stare at them. They were dirty and poorly dressed. Most were thin and sickly looking.

"Looks like they took the beds down round the stove. We'll have to be closer to the door, but let's move down close as we kin git to be closer to the fire. We'll leave this end to other newcomers," Lum suggested, looking around at the Arkansas men.

The Company I men brought their few belongings down to where the Mississippi men were bunked. One of the Rebs there, seated on the lower bunk, got up and ambled over toward the newcomers. The man, slender and tall, had a heavy mustache and a goatee that had grown out to long. He wore a floppy hat with the front of the hat rim bent back up.

"Where you'uns from?" he asked, looking first at David and then at Earl.

"We from Arkansas, David replied, studying the man. "Got captured at Arkansas Post 'bout week ago."

"We didn't hear about that; guess we still losing?" the man asked, now looking over the other Arkansans.

"Back east, Lee's won some good victories, but not in our neck of the woods," spoke Lum, who had already been looking over the barrack for any possible weak places. "Grunt is still trying to take Vicksburg."

"Yeah, he brought down Fort Donelson where we was," the man replied. "Why we are here."

By then most of the new arrivals had sat down on a bunk. Another slender-looking Reb moved up alongside the first speaker.

"Put your belongings under the bottom bunk. We tossed a coin to see who would get the lower level of the bunks. The bed's all 'bout the same — light mattress over board surface — get used to after 'while. Oh, I'm Lieutenant Hobbs," the officer said, glancing around.

"What about the guards; are they watching all the time?" Squirrel asked, looking from one of the men to the other.

A third man, probably about nineteen years old and with no facial hair, had walked up by the first two Mississippi men. He had obviously listened to everything that was said.

"We call them hospital rats, not guards. They never seen any fighting. But with a weapon in their hands, they can be mean and cruel. Gotta watch 'em. They been lot meaner since one was found with his throat cut week or so ago."

There was some laughter from those behind that were listening.

"Durn Yanks never did catch the guilty party."

Again there was more laughter from the group. Suddenly the door opened again and another thirty or forty men soon came inside.

"Rebs will tell you what to do," the guard said as he closed the door.

By nightfall, more than 120 men occupied the barrack, with some spare beds yet to be filled.

Beyond having to provide food for the Union armies, the Federal War department, under Edwin Stanton, now had to provide food for more than twelve different prisoner of war camps. The daily ration for prisoners at Camp Douglas was twelve and a half pounds of beans or peas per 100 rations or eight ounces of rice or hominy per 100 rations and fifteen ounces of potatoes per 100 rations. This usually led to some kind of soup. Occasionally, a small amount of beef or pork would get on a plate.

As the friendships grew between prisoners in the barrack, the later arrivals learned more and more about their captors.

After only a week in the compound, David had already grown thinner and even more depressed.

By then, Lum had developed a short Bible devotion for every evening. There were ten or twelve Bibles in the barrack and the men were quick to share one. One evening in early February, Lum read an account from the Bible where the early New Testament preachers, Paul and Silas, had been beaten and imprisoned. Rather than complain, the two missionaries began to sing and pray throughout the night. Suddenly an act of God opened the prison gates and the two missionaries could have escaped but didn't. The Bible reports that eventually the jailer became a believer and took the two men into his own home until they were set free.

As Lum commented about the account, David realized that he was comparing the story of the first century to the Rebs imprisonment. David thought, I can't believe that story. If it's true, why doesn't this loving God open the gate of this camp? I've heard of better fairytales in my life.

David got up to go to the privy. Later, while walking back to the barrack, he heard singing. As he continued walking back, he thought again about his family back in Bluffton. He hoped his ma was well. What about his old love, Lillie? Was she happy? He hoped that she was very happy — even with children.

When David opened the door to the barrack, he noticed that the men had stopped singing. A small group of men, not far from the stove, was in a close huddle, talking about something. Included in the group were Lum, Squirrel, and Earl. As David walked toward the fire, Lum looked up and motioned for him to join the group. David pulled up an old box to sit on.

"This war will last at least two more years, if not longer," Earl was saying. "Don't know 'bout ya'll, but I'm not ready to stay here that long. We been talkin', and this place has some bad weaknesses. The fence is hardly six feet high cause the camp was originally made for training Federal troops. They's not heavy fence at all and they's not that many guard houses."

"Tell you something else," Lum interrupted. "These hospital rats, one, have old muskets, and two, they never been to battle — bound to be poor shots."

"Well, Lieutenant Hobbs said they have bribed the guards two or three times," interrupted David. "Ain't that right, Lieutenant?"

"We have probably bribed them three or four times," the officer said.

"If everyone agrees, I will pick a committee of six men to plan an escape," Earl resumed talking.

Most of the larger group listening replied with positive comments.

"Yeah."

"You bet."

"Get after it."

Chapter 23

Morgan's Mule

February 1863

MAIL CALL OCCURRED ONCE a week, usually on Fridays. The Arkansans were shocked that the prisoners were allowed to receive money, food, and gifts from their families back home. By then, several of the Mississippi men had already received money from home that they could use in the camp commissary. The Yell County boys quickly wrote letters to their loved ones back home. Since the camp headquarters had confiscated all of the men's money when they entered the camp, the men were surprised to find that they could withdraw funds from their own account for postage costs.

On the last Friday of February, mail call was progressing shortly after 10:00 a.m. The mail guard, as he was called, was calling out the names of those who had received letters. He handed out several letters to the addressees.

"Lofland, David," he then called out. "From Lillie Claxton."

David listened in shock. How could Lillie know of his imprisonment?

"From my former girlfriend," he mentioned, stepping around the waiting men and moving toward the mail clerk.

The mail guard reached out his hand with the letter.

"Ramsey, Bob," he called next. As he did, a Union officer stepped forward and took the letter addressed to David.

"I'm David Lofland," David said to the officer.

"Yes, I know who you are — a real troublemaker. You've been calling my men names — pretty bad names, Lofland. So I will burn your little harlot's precious letter."

He turned to walk away as several guards laughed. Suddenly, David sprinted toward the officer. He was not ready for the tremendous blow, as David landed on his shoulders. As he fell forward with the momentum of David on his back, the officer's face hit the hard surface of the campground — nose first. Quickly, two Union guards rushed over to grab the angry Reb and pull him off the officer.

The shocked officer slowly got to his feet. His nose was smashed and bleeding. He turned and calmly walked back to the struggling Reb soldier, now being tightly held by the guards. He moved up close to David's face, as he wiped the blood off his nose and face with a handkerchief.

"Reb, you will regret that stupid move." He looked to the men holding David, and commanded, "Let Mr. Lofland ride the mule for two hours." He smiled, turned, and walked back toward headquarters still wiping blood from his face.

"What's he mean, ride the mule?" asked Lum, who was standing near one of the Mississippi men.

"It's bad," said the man, turning to look at Lum. "Morgan's Mule — we seen it once for ya'll got here. "Put him straddle a huge sawhorse with weights on his feet — hands tied behind his back. Guy we saw begged and cried for an hour. Poor guy couldn't walk for three days."

Mail call was now over and most of the men that had gathered there moved over to the place where the two guards were taking David. A third guard was struggling to drag a huge replica of a carpenter's sawhorse out of a nearby shed. The top board, a two by four, was nailed at both ends to tripod supports at each end. It was positioned so that the narrow part of the board was on top. The huge sawhorse was twelve feet high.

Another soldier brought a ladder. After tying David's hands behind his back, a guard helped him climb the ladder. He was then hoisted over the narrow one and a half inch wide board. David screamed at landing solidly on the narrow board. Still, another guard brought two wooden buckets. The buckets were tied securely above each ankle. Then each bucket was half-filled with water. The guards then moved the ladder.

David was already in unbelievable pain. Yet, he knew if he did not maintain his balance, he would fall, and with his hands tied behind his back, who knew how many bones could break? David's face grimaced in pain as he moaned out loud. The onlookers noticed tears running down his face. Soon, they all turned away, except for Earl, Squirrel, and Lum. No one wanted to see a human being in such pain. The lone guard paid little attention to David's agony.

"How long?" screamed out David, to his faithful friends who were still there.

"Been ten minutes," Lum shouted. "Pray, Blue! Pray! Ask the Lord for help —he will help you," yelled Lum with tears in his own eyes.

In great pain, David heard the advice. Although barely able to think, he still thought, what do you mean pray? Why didn't your God help before I got here? If there is a God, he hates me. But even in his terrible agony, David was able to recall the mail guard's reference to Lillie. She knew where he was, and she had tried to contact him. How could that be?

And then, he almost lost his balance. Yet, he thought, could that be so bad? Probably, because they would never pick him up, regardless of the number of broken bones.

"Hate!" screamed Squirrel, who was almost crying. "David, use hate! Survive to make them pay! Hate!" David needed no one to tell him to hate. It seemed that much of the world needed to be hated.

After he had gone through the longest two hours of his life and unbelievable pain, it took two ladders and four guards to help David down from the scaffold. Unable to stand, he sank to the ground crying. His three friends had never left David as he struggled to survive the torture.

"Hey, you three men help the Reb inside the barrack," ordered a guard who seemed in sympathy.

With Earl on one side and Lum on the other, the two men supported most of David's weight as they moved him inside the barrack. Once they were inside, all eyes were on David, as his friends carried him to his bunk. He screamed with pain when they carefully laid him on the bed. Once there, he seemed to relax a little, although he could not move. Lum noticed that he had urinated at least once while on the scaffold.

"Blue, can you hear me?" Lum anxiously asked.

"Yow," he muttered.

"We gonna clean your face. If you need to go to the privy, let us know and we'll help. We'll also get you food and help you eat. Do you hear?"

Again, they heard a low, "Yow."

Over the next two weeks, David received the best care that his friends could provide. At the same time, the escape committee was still making plans.

~~~

One of the strangest things that the Arkansans observed

was the appearance of slaves in the camp. Several Confederate officers had been captured, along with their black servants. The camp officials included the slaves on the camp rolls. For the most part, the Union guards and officers were very prejudiced against blacks. They resented black prisoners, perhaps more than white prisoners.

One evening, after Lum had helped David go to the privy, he and Squirrel went out into the prison yard. Late February was showing some sign of springtime. As the two friends walked around the facility, they noticed one of the black prisoners walking near the dead line. The white prisoners would usually get a warning from the guards in the guard tower if they got too close to the dead line. As the two walked along, talking about a breakout scheme, they heard a shot behind them. Both men whirled around to see a young black slave fall to the ground.

"Hey, he wasn't over the line!" screamed Lum at the guard tower.

"Johnnie, your eyes are bad," shouted the guard. "Mind your own business, scum."

Several Chicago sightseers from the city now arrived every day. A special platform was built outside the prison wall so that they could come and view the Southern rabble. The cost was ten cents. As the weather grew warmer, more and more people came to view the captured enemy.

Many of the Chicago people proved to be sympathetic toward the prisoners. A benevolent fund was soon established to purchase clothing for them. People from the local churches began visiting the prison, and before long outsiders had established a Bible study.

David had been out of bed for a week when he was invited to the new Bible study in the barracks. He agreed to go for two reasons. One, it was a cool evening, with the north wind really blowing across Lake Michigan, and two, the friends who had nursed him back to health were the ones that had extended the invitation.

The men gathered for the Bible study at the far end of the building near the big wood stove. They chattered and joked until Lum finally introduced the speaker. He referred to the man, a preacher at a local church in Chicago, as Dwight L. Moody. After some lighthearted stories, Moody began to warm up. It turned out to be the typical fire and brimstone sermon preached a lot during wartime. David could not help listening some, and he had to admit, it was a well-presented sermon. At the close of the service, the preacher issued an altar call. More than twenty men went forward to make decisions of some kind.

Chapter 24

Escape

THE ESCAPE PLAN WAS ready. The plan called for someone to crawl through a hole in the barrack floor and then out from under the barrack, which was almost two feet off the ground on blocks. The man would then move over to the tall shed where the Morgan's Mule scaffold was stored and set fire to flammable materials inside the shed. They hoped that the shed and the wooden mule would both burn. While the fire was burning, the men involved would break for the fence on the opposite side of the camp and hopefully scale it during the turmoil created by the fire. The question was who was small enough to go through the hole created in the floor. Squirrel immediately volunteered for the task.

Lum had been storing away flammable materials for more than two months. There was also enough flint stone to start a fire. Everything was ready when the designated escape day arrived.

"Squirrel, maybe more moonlight tonight," Lum said. "If so, creep along in the shadow of the building. If they see ya, run and throw your flint away. Tell them you were going to the privy. Above all, don't stay long in the shed. When they see light or a fire, they will come in a hurry. Get back here quickly. While the excitement is going on, we will try to enlarge the hole in the floor. We will hit the west wall on the other side of barrack 86. Got it??

"Should — third time you told me," Squirrel said in an irritated manner.

As the night darkened, the men talked about what they would do once outside the wall.

"Eventually, the train or a ship might work, but first, get outside and away before they find we are gone," exclaimed Lum, looking around at the group.

"What you think they'll do to us if they catch us?" asked one of the Mississippi soldiers.

"Either shoot us, Morgan's Mule, or the dungeon," replied Earl. "Course, the dungeon's full now from that bribe scandal."

"Hey, they can shoot me," David said. "I'm not riding that mule again. I'm still sore from that."

"And you never broke him," Squirrel said with a grin.

All candles were out by 10:00 p.m. and barrack 87 was quiet. By 11:00 p.m., Squirrel was squeezing through the hole in the floor. He had some paper and a lot of wood chips stuffed in his pockets, along with the flint. The sky had a few clouds, so the moon would be partially concealed at times. Squirrel crawled through the hole in the floor and then beneath the floor of the barrack and over to the edge of the building. There was a shadow now between barrack 87 and 88, cast by barrack 88.

He crawled under barrack 88 and then beneath three more barracks. He finally got to the last building closest to the east wall. From the barrack, it was about twenty feet over to the mule shed, as the men called the tall building. Even in the dim moonlight, he worried about crossing those twenty feet to the shed. Looking out from under the last barrack, Squirrel took a deep breath and slowly crawled out from under it. He again glanced all around. He could see one guard tower about fifty yards away. The other tower that he worried about was about seventy yards in the other direction. At any minute, he expected to hear a Union officer scream, or worse, catch a musket ball from one of the guard towers. He remembered seeing the young black slave being shot without a warning.

When he had reached the shed, Squirrel heard a noise. Had he been seen? Then he realized that bats, apparently using the shed for roost and shelter, had created the noise. He slowly opened the door of the shed, expecting the old hinge to squeak. He carefully moved inside and waited. After some difficulty, he was able to light a small candle. With it, he looked around the shed. Other than the huge wooden mule, there were a couple of wooden barrels, a ladder, a partial roll of tar paper, and a few old boards.

He took the old, dried paper out of his pocket and placed it close to the old boards. He placed the two pocketfuls of wood chips and wood shavings on the paper. He lowered the candle to the shavings and soon produced a small flame. Squirrel blew softly on the flame, which was soon about six inches high. He adjusted one of the old boards on the flame. The fire was also burning near the base of one of the mule legs. He was sure that the old wood shack would catch fire easily.

He turned and slowly opened the door of the shed. Then he quietly knelt down and began to crawl back toward the nearest barrack. Once he had crawled under the barrack, Squirrel turned to glance back at the shed. He could see the light of the fire through the cracks between the boards. He turned and began to crawl back in the direction of his barrack. There was still no alarm. Finally, after crawling under the floor of his barrack, Squirrel reached the hole in the floor above.

"How'd it go?" whispered David.

"It's burning and that shed is against the fence; if they don't see the fire in minute or two, it will get pretty big," announced Squirrel. "Ya'll ready to go?"

"Well, we can't jerk these boards off till there's some noise," David whispered back.

Then they heard loud voices — and someone rang the fire bell. Squirrel moved back from the hole as the men above jerked a couple of the boards off the flooring.

"That's big enough," Squirrel heard someone say.

David's head came first, and then his upper body. Then he reached down to touch the ground with his hands. He walked on them until his body was completely through the hole. The bell was still ringing, and Squirrel could hear the sounds of men running and talking loudly.

"Get water buckets at the mess hall," someone screamed.

"Get the men out of that first barrack," came another voice.

By then all seven of the escape committee members were through the hole in the floor and over under the edge of the building. Squirrel leading, dashed across the space between the two barracks and immediately went under the adjacent barrack floor. This continued until each man got to the last barrack close to the west wall. By then, every man's attention in the camp was directed on the growing fire. The wood fence by the shed had now begun to burn. As the seven men lay on the ground under the last barrack, Lum repeated the final instructions.

"You first five, go straight from here for the fence. We are between the guard towers, but don't make any noise — just get over."

Earl went first. He sprinted over the thirty feet to the fence and stopped at the base of it. David was right behind him. Earl clasped his hands together and made a step. David put his foot in the step, lunged upward, and grabbed the top of the fence.

With a shove from below, David was over it. There he waited to help the others.

Lum, still on the inside, was helping the others. Five men were soon over the fence and outside. As Lum tried to help the shorter Squirrel, they began to hear whistles in the camp. The guards must have discovered the escape.

David heard loud voices — something about going over the fence. As Squirrel's hands got to the top of it, two guards ran up to him and Lum, out of breath, their guns ready. Realizing what was taking place, David turned to the other four men.

"Run, guards are here," he told the others.

The four men on the outside took off running. The guard near the tower fired one, and then a second shot. One of the running men fell, as the other three continued to run. Another shot rang out, hitting Charles Murphy. The moonlit night must have helped the shooter's aim.

"Stay there, Reb or you are dead," yelled someone. David took it to be him they were talking about.

"Hey, Reb, on the outside, grab that fence and come back over here, less'n you want these two to die," ordered someone from inside the compound.

After a pause, David grabbed the top of the fence, leaped off the ground, pulled himself up to the top of the fence, and dropped down back on the inside of the camp. As demonstrated by the sounds of hounds trailing, the camp security force had finally reacted. The two guards looked at the three Rebs.

"How many got away?" asked the closest guard.

"Bout twenty, I reckon," lied Lum.

"What about Murphy?" asked David, looking at the guard that had spoken. "He was shot."

"We'll let the hounds chew on him awhile."

"All right, down to the guardhouse. Captain will decide what to do with ya'll tomorrow," stated the larger of the two guards.

The guardhouse was a former horse barn, approximately thirty feet by thirty feet. Consequently, there was no heat in the building. After hearing a lock snap shut on the outside, the three men sat down on the ground.

"Wonder if Murphy is dead?" David asked. "Those scumbags wouldn't even go out to help him, but he's probably the luckiest one of the bunch."

"Maybe Earl and the others made it — if the hounds don't track 'em down," surmised Lum, looking at the other two in the dark.

"Hey, I gonna pray for Murphy and the others," Lum said.

David neither bowed nor prayed. He thought, when do these guys give up? Their so-called God has never answered a single prayer. Does God demand prayers only when things go bad? If we planned a little better and prayed less, we'd be lot better off.

Lum was just concluding his prayer. "And we pray the Yanks won't put us on the mule. Amen."

I'll go along with that all right, thought David.

At about 10:00 a.m., a guard on the outside began to take the lock from the door clasp. David could hear voices as well. A guard opened the door and roughly shoved two men into the barn and on the ground. He then slammed the door and snapped the lock shut. Earl and Reuben Strong slowly sat up. Both had bruises and cut marks all over their face. Reuben had a terrible cut on his right forearm.

"They get Hobbs?" David softly asked.

Earl looked so tired that he appeared sick.

"Yeah, shot him. He's dead. Guess Murphy's dead too. Know he was shot as we ran after crossing the fence."

"Well what happened to you guys?" David asked, glancing from one man to the other.

"We got 'bout two mile, I reckon, for the dogs got to us," said Earl, looking up at David and shaking his head in disappointment. "There were five of 'em, meaner'n heck. They didn't just bark — they tore into both of us. Look at Reuben's arm; we tried to fight 'em off, but when the Yanks got there, they just stood and laughed. I picked up a big rock and smashed the head of a big Redbone. Think I killed 'em. That's when the hospital rats waded in with their gun butts. They beat us half to death on the ground. For while, thought they wanted to kill us. Then one of the officers got there and pulled them off. Got dog teeth marks all over — so's Reuben."

"Didn't beat ya'll?" Reuben said, looking up at David.

David hated to admit that they hadn't been punished. "Not yet anyway," he replied, looking at the bite marks on Reuben's face.

The five men sat and talked about their ordeal for an hour or more. The big question was, had it been a sound escape plan and had they cost two brave friends their lives? Near twelve o'clock, guards brought some terrible smelling soup with a piece of tough meat in it. After eating some of the soup, Lum pulled a piece of meat out of the bowl and threw it at the door.

"That meat's rotten," he observed. "Don't eat it."

The other men also threw out the meat that was in their bowls, but hunger caused them to finish the rest of the soup. They soon heard someone removing the door lock again. Four hospital rats were standing there with their guns.

"Captain Mulligan has passed sentence on the prisoners," the short, heavy guard addressed the men. "You will serve two weeks in the White Oak. Come with us."

Chapter 25

White Oak

BY THEN, THEY ALL had heard of the White Oak. It was an underground prison cell made of white oak logs twelve or fourteen inches in diameter. The top of the dungeon extended about one and a half feet above ground level. At the back end and above the surface of the ground was a small window. A trapdoor was the only entrance and exit. From the trapdoor there were ten steps down to the bottom of the dungeon. The floor of the room was clay. With only the small eight by eight inch window, the room was totally dark.

The dungeon could accommodate as many as eight men cramped together in close quarters. Prisoners in White Oak were given one meal per day. With no room, there was no provision for excretion of urine or solid waste. In the summer months, the temperature frequently reached close to 115 degrees in White Oak. The winter was as bad or worse.

The five prisoners followed the guards to the southwest corner of the prison yard. There was the much talked about and much feared dungeon. The first guard used a pulley apparatus to raise the trapdoor and the heavy weight on top of the door. As David glanced down into the dark hole, he thought, it can't be as bad as Morgan's Mule. He started down the steps first. When he got to the clay bottom, he felt around in the dark for a bench or seat of some kind. There was none. He moved over to the back side of the small room, about twelve feet away. The others were descending the steps into White Oak.

"Enjoy," one of the guards said, after Squirrel got to the bottom of the dungeon. Then the heavy door and weight came down with a slam. The men could not see one another in the pitch black, and only now did they begin to notice the terrible stench. The smell seemed to be one of sweat, urine, and feces. No one spoke for seconds.

"Rebs — can you handle it?" asked Lum.

"If the Yankee scum can build it, we can stand it," answered Earl.

The day slowly passed, and the men talked less and less. Most had begun to think about themselves. Could they survive two weeks in this pitch-black room? What about excretion and the need to urinate? Was there enough room to lie down and try to sleep? Who came up with the stupid idea of escape anyway?

After two hours, there was little conversation between the captives. If talking occurred, it was usually negative conversation.

"We were crazy to try such a poorly planned escape," Reuben said, directing some criticism toward Lum, who was responsible for much of the planning.

"Murphy pushed a lot of it," Earl said, casting blame on Charles Murphy, who had been killed in the escape attempt.

No one spoke again for some time. Lum, listening to the earlier comments, had been thinking. To him, the men's attitudes were already breaking down. As a leader, he knew he could not let his friends lose hope and begin to attack each other. He had already begun to think about some way to combat this darkened pit of isolation. But he also knew that he must convince the men that positive conversation was necessary.

As he sat there, Lum thought, a man could go mad in such a place, especially if he was alone. He felt they were blessed to have friends in the dungeon with them. As the conversation almost completely stopped, Lum continued to think. We gotta be creative, gotta talk — tell stories. Need to pray, even sing. We could even have each person tell his life story. After that, each man could explain what he wanted to accomplish in life. If necessary, we could make up stories, anything to preserve our sanity, Lum thought. Finally, Lum was ready to speak.

"Men, want you to listen to me — gonna preach awhile."

David thought, surely not yet.

"Men, people go crazy in dark, isolated places like this. You can give up to being crazy, but not me."

"Me neither," someone said.

"We have got to beat this pit of dark isolation."

"How?" interrupted Squirrel.

"We have got to talk, tell about ourselves, 'bout our families. Tell who we are, or what we hope to be. Have an idea — we gonna play a game if ya'll will go along."

"Sounds okay," Earl said, glancing around as if he could see his friends.

"Blue?" questioned Lum.

"Okay with me," he replied.

"Okay, first, we sing, 'Dixie.' A one and a two — Oh, I...'"

After they finished the song, Lum looked in the direction to where Reuben was sitting.

"Now, Reuben, tell everyone all the animals that live on your father's farm, along with a count of each."

Four hours went by as the men answered all kinds of questions about their homes and growing up. Eventually, the group concluded from observing the small window that nightfall had arrived. Lum, by then the accepted leader, suggested a prayer.

"I will volunteer tonight and so on. Would you bow with me?"

David thought Lum would never stop praying. He was as bad as old man Rader, and David could not agree with much of the prayer. Why would he thank God for blessing them so — the escape failed, two men were killed, they were eating rotten meat, and now they were in a real hell hole. These were blessings? David thought, if these are blessings, I've been blessed a lot since leaving Tennessee. His thoughts were interrupted as he noticed Lum was still praying.

"And thank you that Blue survived Morgan's Mule."

David thought, why didn't he help me avoid the mule? Besides, he thought, most people probably survive the mule. Lum was finishing up his prayer. "In Jesus' name. Amen."

After the first week in the dungeon, the men were doing okay mentally due to Lum's constant prodding. But there were other serious problems. Each man had at least two bowel movements and they had urinated several times, all in their clothes. The place smelled horrible and Reuben was already quite ill. Even though short-tempered and cranky, the men were surviving.

The most important part of each day was when a guard brought the lone meal and water to White Oak. Each day, a different man was selected to go to the top step, look out, and get the prepared food. With no light at all, when the men ate, they learned the menu through taste alone. Regardless, they ate the food quickly, with no complaints.

With the feces-covered clothes, and the smell, things grew worse the second week. Lum was also about to exhaust the topic list that the men could discuss. On one occasion, David almost got into a fight with Earl over space on the floor. Lum had to step in and cool tempers.

With two days left, Lum had another idea of what to discuss. Why not religion, he thought; after all, we do pray every day. He had noticed that David was the only one of the five that had not volunteered to pray. He wondered why that was so.

"Okay, men, our discussion topic this afternoon is religion. If you would, please tell us about your faith and what part God plays in your life. Be good if each of us could assume an hour talking about our faith. All right, let's begin with Squirrel."

Almost three hours later, after Squirrel, Earl, and Lum had quite fully answered the religious question, Lum called on David. He was worried whether David would participate at all. There was a brief pause. However, David hated not to do his share to prevent the mind-killing boredom that infected the little group. He had certainly seen evidence that Lum's idea was succeeding.

"Well, I's raised in Christian home. We went to church a lot. Ma and Pa talked about God quite a bit. Reckon I was saved — 'bout nine years old, and I was baptized in a creek in North Carolina. I believed in God for a long time, probably up until 'bout eighteen. At the time, I's in a Sunday school class with a girl, Lillie — beautiful girl."

David continued to tell of his losing Lillie to the preacher and leaving Tennessee. He mentioned Becky's attempt to drown herself, the slave auction, and the black revival. He told of his father's murder. After a full hour of talking, David ended with his ride on Morgan's Mule and the present stay in White Oak.

"Men, not sure they's a God; wouldn't he offer a little help once in awhile? I didn't quit believing all at once — been over a period of three years or so. Now, I don't mind ya'll praying and reading the Bible — even hope we get some help. Reckon that's all."

No one spoke for several seconds. Then Lum called on Reuben. The lone Mississippi man gave an impressive account of his religious life as a member of a large family of twelve. After the finish, Lum thanked all four of the men for contributing to the conversation.

"Not only did we kill a lot of time, but we learned a lot about each other. Men, I love you all and we gonna make it — mark my word. We got help from above."

As the men relaxed against the clay embankment ten feet below ground level, David thought about Lum's words. No doubt, Lum's ideas on forced conversation had really helped them pass time in the dungeon. At the same time, he knew his friends so much better now, because they had shared private things that they never would have mentioned about their lives. He admired Lum a lot for thinking of all five of the men rather than just himself. He wondered why Lum was so thoughtful.

The next morning, all realized it was the final day in White Oak dungeon. There was even some light-hearted joking about Lum's snoring and David's talking in his sleep.

"That Lillie must have been som'in, David," Earl said to his friend.

"Did I talk 'bout her ag'in last night? That was the night before," David said as he defended himself.

"Oh, no," interjected Squirrel, "You's talking 'bout her ag'in last night too."

"Don't know how you could hear me with Lum's braying. Lum, you could get a job on a paddle wheeler as the horn," David said.

They all laughed.

"Dreamed I was six foot tall and all the girls were fightin' over me. Couldn't even pick one, they's so many," Squirrel said as they all laughed.

"Good lands, Squirrel, you'ed had to grow two feet," David said, nudging Squirrel, who was sitting on the ground by him.

Again they all laughed.

"Think we ought to pick the smelliest one of us before we get out?" the quieter Reuben asked.

"I vote Reuben."

"I'd say Reuben."

"No doubt, Reuben."

"Got to be Reuben," came the fourth vote.

"Reckon I vote for Reuben too," Reuben jokingly replied as all five men laughed.

"Well, means I will git the first bath anyway," Reuben said as the men laughed again.

On the outside, four Union guards were standing near the trapdoor ready to raise it and help the survivors out of White Oak.

"You hear them? They's been laughing for last five minutes. Never seen that before," the officer in the group stated.

The heavy door slowly rose. At least 200 Rebs from the camp were standing close by watching. And then from the bottom of the dungeon, the watchers heard, "Oh, I wish I was in the land of cotton, all things there not forgotten — look away, look away."

The blue-clad guards stood there with their mouths open. Behind the amazed onlookers, the 200 Reb prisoners joined in on the beloved Southern song — "look away, look away, Dixieland."

Men at other locations in the camp could now hear the voices of their comrades singing. Soon, the whole camp seemed to be singing together.

Chapter 26

Hunger

March 1863

DAVID HAD NEVER FELT so good, after being allowed to bathe. As he slowly dressed into his other change of clothing, he thought about the ordeal in White Oak. Other men had told him that the captives placed in the dungeon often went insane. Some had died in the terrible hole. A thought — did they receive some divine assistance? If they had, must be a God. He would have to give this more thought.

On Friday, all prisoners had to go through the normal delousing procedure. They had all been required to go through the routine several times. After removing all clothing, the prisoners had to walk down an incline into a pool of smelly, green liquid. They were required to dunk their head completely under the surface of the fluid at least once before climbing up the incline on the other side of the wooden tank. Some prisoners thought the delousing procedure was effective, while others even believed that the terrible smelling fluid even attracted more lice.

In mid–March, the Reb prisoners faced another problem. Earlier that month, the camp commander, General Hoffman, had stopped supplying fresh vegetables to the prisoners. Any purchased vegetables went to the camp hospital or to the officers' mess. Later in March, several prisoners became ill. In a short time, several men died before it was determined that the spreading disease was scurvy. Forty-two men died that month, and still Hoffman refused to order fresh vegetables.

Squirrel and Reuben both came down seriously ill. When it was decided that the two men were sick enough, they were transferred to the camp hospital. Reuben, who had been sick awhile in White Oak, died three days later. The remaining members of the dungeon group worried and prayed about the smallest Reb in barrack 87. Lum had called a prayer meeting when the two men were removed to the camp hospital. The men had prayed fervently each evening before they went to bed. At one of the first prayer meetings, Earl noticed that David had bowed his head during the prayer. After Reuben passed, and Squirrel's condition grew worse, the men's prayers increased in intensity.

During this same time, the camp rations were cut yet again. Oney Taylor, Company I adjutant, made a formal complaint to Hoffman, the camp commander. Taylor said that soldiers deserved more food, especially vegetables, in order to prevent scurvy. He also explained that it was not so much the quality of the food as it was the quantity.

Hoffman resented the formal complaint.

"Reb, you know what your men are feeding our men at Andersonville?" he said, glaring angrily back at the adjutant. "About half of what ya'll are getting. Either live with it or die from it. Now get back to your treasonous Rebs."

The next day, the men in barrack 87 began trying to catch some of the healthy rats that had infested the building. When told about the extra ration of rat, David vowed that he would never eat one. Four days later, he enjoyed part of a big rat that

Earl had caught in a homemade trap. Rats became a frequent supplement to the prisoner's diet.

Late in March 1863, due to complaints made by several of the sympathetic people of Chicago, the Chicago Tribune demanded in an editorial that the government provide a team of doctors to examine conditions at Camp Douglas. Because of the public pressure, doctors were selected to investigate the camp and submit a detailed report. The Tribune was finally able to get a copy of the report. The doctors reported that the facility was an extermination camp. They stated that there was little or no bedding for the inmates and that the camp was covered with lice and other vermin. Finally, they reported that 800 men had died within the last ninety days. The Tribune, a strong voice for President Lincoln, called the camp conditions ridiculous.

The food content in the camp improved some after the newspaper report. Also, the sympathetic people of Chicago donated more clothes to the camp.

Chapter 27

The Bribe

MARCH 1863 CAME IN with a heavy rain and another fifty Reb prisoners. The new arrivals were assigned bunks in barrack 74. When David and Lum saw a foursome standing outside their barrack later on, they decided to visit with them and find out how the war was going.

"Welcome to the worst place this side of hell," Lum said with a grin, as they approached the men. "Where ya'll from?"

A tall, heavy Reb standing with the use of a homemade crutch looked at them suspiciously.

"We's part of John Hunt Morgan's Cavalry. Got captured in Kentucky, but we'd won the battle. How 'bout you'uns?"

"We Arkys — captured at Arkansas Post. Been here since late January," Lum answered, looking over the cavalrymen. He thought that the men looked a cut above most of the infantrymen that had been sent to the camp.

"Ya'll tried to break out yet?" asked another man, who looked to be an officer.

"Been couple hundred broke out, but most have been shot or died as a result of Yankee torture," David replied.

By then, four or five more of the newcomers had walked up to the group.

"Guards tough?" asked one of the men who had arrived late.

"Hospital rats — they never seen battle. But, with a loaded gun, they can be mean," responded Lum, looking at the men who had just walked up to the group.

"Well, we'll break out in week's time," said the big man, who was apparently a leader.

"Much as I hate to say it, welcome to Douglas," Lum said as soon as the Kentucky men turned to look around at their new home.

The next day, the camp staff informed each barrack that smallpox had hit the camp in a very aggressive way. It was soon announced that 102 men had already died from the disease. Squirrel, much better now, was released from the hospital so that a smallpox victim could have his bed.

Within three days, more than forty men in barrack 87 had died. The Union medical staff did not seem to know how to deal with the new epidemic. Within another week, there were only thirty-one men left in barrack 87. The Arky men were now as thin and emaciated as most of the men in the other barracks.

By the third week of March, John Hunt Morgan's men had worked out an escape plan. They had enlisted the services of one of the Union guards. The Rebs had seen Private Harsworth, a recent arrival from Ohio, walk to the guard tower in the evenings to report for the graveyard shift several times. One of Morgan's men eventually approached the Federal private and asked if he would be interested in making some money.

"I might, especially being on the pay of a private. Besides, I been thinking 'bout leaving this hellhole. I've had enough," the man said, looking at the Reb contact.

"What about if it involved an escape?" the Reb asked.

"Look, Reb, for fifty bucks I'd overlook twenty escapees. That would get me to Cleveland."

After two more meetings, the contact, Rod Williams, was sure that Harsworth would go along with the escape. With a third visit, Private Harsworth assured Williams that a guard in tower four would also go along, for twenty–five dollars. With the assurance of Williams, the escape committee made plans for the break.

Then men drew straws to choose fifteen men from Hunt's cavalry contingent. To pay off the Union guard, several members of the Hunt group requested and received money from their families. They barely reached the seventy-five dollars needed to fund the escape project.

The cavalry unit had planned the escape for the last Saturday in March. They chose that day of the week since the camp guards were usually lax on weekends — sometimes because of their use of alcoholic beverages.

David and Lum had been informed of the escape, since they had planned the earlier failed escape. On the chosen Saturday, Williams again verified with Harsworth that the fifteen men could cross the fence around 1:00 a.m. Harsworth reported that he had paid the second Union guard his twenty-five dollars and he had agreed to ignore the escapees. The fifteen men involved were fully prepared, knowing that they had a chance to get several miles away before camp officials noticed the escape. Everyone in barrack 74 was excited for the men.

Just before 1:00 a.m., the men began to let themselves down through a hole in the floor of the building. In their barrack, David and Lum waited, hoping the escape would be successful. By one o'clock, the fifteen men had reached the fence. Slowly and quietly, ten of the men scaled the fence in the dim moonlight. They were unaware that on the outside of the fence, approximately fifty feet away and behind a small building, stood one of the new army Gatling guns. Suddenly, the new, quick-firing gun opened up on the Rebs outside the fence, hitting each man at least twice. On the inside of the fence, four Union soldiers stepped out from behind both ends of the barrack.

"Hands up, Rebs!" shouted an officer. "Your scheme has failed."

As the Rebs turned to face the armed guards, Rob Williams looked up at the guard tower, wondering how they had been betrayed. He could not see Harsworth, who was smiling as he counted his seventy-five dollars.

When they heard the rapid fire of the Gatling gun, David and Lum knew that Harsworth had set up Hunt's men. Two days later, four of the remaining five men who had attempted to escape were sent to the White Oak for two weeks. Harsworth swore that the Rebs — in particular, Rod Williams — had tried to bribe him, but that he had declined the money. Williams tried to convince the Union officers that Harsworth had taken the money, but they weren't willing to believe a Reb's word. Williams was charged with attempting to bribe a Union soldier. His sentence was to be hanged.

The guards forced all of the prisoners in the camp to come out and watch the first hanging in more than two months. They tied the sentenced Reb's hands behind his back, placed a blindfold over his eyes, and hoisted him up on a barrel about three feet high. Mulligan, the camp commander, made some comments about prisoners obeying camp rules, and a guard kicked the barrel out from under the victim. The drop to the ground, unfortunately, was not far enough to break the Reb's neck. He hung there for three or four minutes, slowly choking to death. As the prisoners observed the execution, the watchers whispered numerous curses and threats.

"To die is one thing, but to be tortured to death is something else," said David, watching the still-kicking legs of the dying Reb. "I hate em with a passion."

"Know what you mean," agreed Lum.

Two nights later, someone found Private Harsworth in the guard's tower with his throat cut. His empty wallet was on his chest. They never found the murderer. Even the Rebs, talking among themselves, concluded that it would take a squirrel to scale the steep tower supports to kill the man.

The question now among the Rebs was if smallpox was the worst problem or if hunger was the greatest concern. By then, all the prisoners were thin and sickly. An occasional rat kept some of the Rebs alive.

Lieutenant O'Hare, a friendly Union officer, had a pet spaniel. The little red dog was a favorite among the guards, as well as the Reb prisoners. He was allowed to run and play with the prisoners while the lieutenant was making his daily rounds. One day the dog went missing. A couple of days later, the lieutenant posted a notice on the big, camp bulletin board about the missing dog. The next morning there was a second notice posted on the backside of the lieutenant's notice: "Yankees — for want of bread, the dog is dead, for want of meat, the dog was eat."

An investigation occurred for a full day in an effort to find any evidence as to who took the dog. Nothing was ever uncovered.

Chapter 28

The Tunnel

March 1863

NOT LONG AFTER THE two attempted escapes through the barrack flooring, Camp Douglas officials decided to enclose the foundations of the barracks. While prisoners of war were not supposed to be forced to work, more than 200 Rebs were placed on the work detail to build solid foundations underneath the camp barracks. While the new foundations would provide more security for the barracks, camp officials gave little thought to the possible new avenue of escape that the enclosed foundations would present to the prisoners of war. One, items, even weapons, could be hidden under the flooring, and two, there was a much better chance now to consider building a tunnel underneath the barrack and on outside the camp. Even before the enclosed foundations were complete, plans were underway to create a tunnel under the flooring, under the foundations, and eventually, under the fence.

With the recent discovery of the escape attempt by barrack 87 and the men's sentence to White Oak, Lum did not feel that the men in barrack 87 should get involved in another escape attempt so soon. However, he was asked to offer advice about another escape, this one involving a tunnel. He met several times with two prisoners from barrack 61, a barrack located near the camp fence. After listening to the proposed escape plan, Lum suggested one change. He recommended that the men in barrack 61 create two holes under the flooring.

"Dig a hole and partial tunnel for about eight feet. Then select the second place for the real tunnel," he told the men. "If the guards get suspicious, allow them to discover the first tunnel. That will take the heat off any other tunneling."

"What we do with the dirt from the tunnel?" asked one of the Rebs, an officer with protruding front teeth.

"Hey, we'll come over tonight after mess and see if we can git ya going," Lum suggested as he continued to survey the building.

After supper, the four Arkys went over to barrack 61. Along with six men from that barrack, the Yell County men took seats in a far corner. Lum began by introducing his four friends.

"First, boys, we already failed in a breakout — got two friends killed in doing it. But I wish we could have tried to tunnel out. Course, then they was not a solid foundation," he then reported, looking around the group. "Since ya'll's mentioned it, I've done some thinking about it. As I told you'uns other day," he said, looking at the two men that had contacted him, "I'd make a false hole, not very big, and a real hole — different ends of the barrack. The real hole ought to be in a, what they say, less conspicuous place than the false hole. Won't take any longer to have two holes — you got plenty enough men."

Gary Simpson, the barrack 61 leader, again asked about all the dirt coming from the tunnels.

"Look, the foundation is almost two feet high," said David, who had been listening. "Got plenty of room to move the digged dirt back around the foundation all on the other side."

"Sure," agreed Earl. "Have one group of diggers under

the floor and another group to scatter the dirt around the foundation on the other side of the building.

"All sounds good," Squirrel said, "but most important is to have bunch of men watching for guards — at all times. And you can't have no rats in your barrack that will give you away."

"Don't have to worry about rats," said a dark-complexioned man, standing near the group. "We's already eat 'em all."

The group laughed as Lum resumed talking.

"Watch for men from other barracks, or strangers — guards can also dress up like us and come on in. Need signals and signs to warn you of any people you don't know. I'd also be careful about getting too dirty down in the tunnel and then going out where the hospital rats can see you. They might figure out what going on."

"Believe I'd do most of the digging at dark," David suggested. "Course, you may use all your candles, but we can try to borrow candles from other barracks — don't ya'll ask for any candles."

"How long you reckon it will take on the real tunnel?" Simpson spoke again.

"Hard to say; if we get another heavy freeze, ground's going to be awful hard," Lum said, staring at the wood stove in the corner. "Simpson, put the real tunnel 'bout ten feet or so from the stove by the wall. Stove'll give the digger below some heat from above and there's always lot of extra dirt around a stove, with dirt coming off the logs."

"You might keep the extra fire logs over your board hole down below," offered David.

"Good idea," one of the men said.

"Ya'll got a shovel?" Squirrel asked.

"We stoled two shovels and a hoe while on the work detail to enclose the foundation," a third man said. "Under the floor already."

"Okay, men, we'll use our contacts to get extra candles for you," Lum said. "Also keep our eyes open for anything else to dig with. Could send Squirrel downtown Chicago to buy shovels, but he'd run off with the first woman he met that was under four feet tall."

Everyone laughed except the short Squirrel, who gave Lum a dirty look.

Two days later, with six extra candles, Simpson got the project underway. Squirrel was the only outsider to be included in the tunnel project. His small size made him an attractive candidate for building a tunnel.

Each day, Lum would get a report from "Mole" about the progress of the tunnel. After a week, one of the guards began to notice that Squirrel went to barrack 61 every day, spent a lot of time, and came back to his barrack quite dirty. Surveillance began and continued for several days before a guard, dressed as a prisoner, ambled into barrack 61 and looked around.

The undercover guard, nosing around the barrack, came upon a suspicious corner where several men were sitting. He also noticed an unusual amount of dirt in the area. He left the barrack and ultimately made a report about the suspicious developments in barrack 61. Two days later, ten guards arrived at the barrack to investigate. The Reb lookouts were fortunate to be able to alert everyone in the barrack and get everyone out of the tunnel before the guards could uncover the scheme.

The hospital rats discovered a short tunnel that appeared to be the start of a serious breakout tunnel. That evening, guards closed barrack 61 and began a serious investigation. They questioned all residents of the barrack in private about the project. They also brought Squirrel over for questioning. Yet, none of the Rebs seemed to know anything about the project.

The interrogation continued throughout the next day. With

no information to go on, Mulligan threatened to punish everyone in the barrack, including Squirrel, unless an informant stepped forward.

"Over hundred men — not going to shoot that many," Squirrel said that evening as he told his friends about the commander's threats. "Too many for White Oak — or the Mule."

"Squirrel, they could use the Gatling gun on that many," Earl offered.

"Well, no one escaped, so the punishment may not be so bad," David said.

The investigation continued the following day. A staff officer that the prisoners had only seen a time or two addressed the Rebs in barrack 61.

"Rebs, we ought to hang everyone in here — you all are guilty. I will give you one last chance to avoid group punishment. Who led this scheme?"

Squirrel anxiously looked around, wondering if there were any uneaten rats left. No one spoke. The officer was now frowning and shaking his head.

"Rebs, it is ten degrees below zero outside and there is four inches of snow on the ground. How long could you stand it outside with no coat — and no shoes?" He glared around the barrack at the Rebs.

"Okay, everyone take off your shoes — and socks. Please move outside," the angry officer said in an irritated manner.

Once outside, the men were put into five rows, with twenty men in each row — arm's length apart. The icy temperature and the snow were already affecting the men's bare feet.

"You will all stand in the snow on your bare right foot as you hold your left leg in your left hand behind you," the captain commanded, glaring at the group of more than one hundred men. "You lower that left leg to the ground and you will catch a rifle butt. Okay, on your right foot, left leg up in your left hand."

All the Rebs complied, although some were jumping around a little, trying to keep their balance. Within fifteen minutes, the guards had struck several Rebs for lowering their left leg. Within thirty minutes, several men had leg calf muscles that were severely cramping; they were forced to get relief by putting weight on the left leg. With the relief came a rifle blow from the guards. Squirrel, who didn't seem to have much muscle, seemed to handle the discomfort quite well. As he glanced around, it looked like at least half of the men were on the ground being beaten by the guards.

At the end of the hour, Squirrel and one other young Reb were the only men standing upright. The guards released Squirrel and the other man from further punishment, but they forced all the others to stand thirty more minutes on their left leg. As the two walked back to the barrack, Squirrel looked over at the other man.

"Let's get back inside and work on the real tunnel," he said.

Three nights later, twenty men escaped through the "real" tunnel. Since the escape was at night, Squirrel could not be part of the escape.

Two weeks later, Squirrel received a letter from St. Louis. It was from the young Reb who had survived the one–legged punishment with him in the snow. He was one of the prisoners who escaped through the tunnel. With the letter he sent Squirrel twenty dollars. Although he didn't say why he sent it, Squirrel knew it was in appreciation for all his help. Squirrel sent fifteen dollars to his family. When the other men found out that he had mailed the money back home, they were impressed with his unselfish attitude.

"To buy big Glenda that wedding dress afore Lum gits home to marry her," Squirrel said. "Everyone in Nola knows she's been promised to Lum."

Even Lum laughed at the little guy's humor.

Chapter 29

Prisoner Exchange

April 1863

ON APRIL 3, AROUND 9:00 a.m., a Union officer entered barrack number 87. All the men in the barrack looked toward the officer, who seemed ready to make an important announcement.

"Rebs, General Halleck has approved a prisoner exchange with the Reb government. Three hundred of you prisoners that have been here the longest will be sent to City Point, Virginia, where you will be exchanged for Union prisoners that are being held in Confederate prison camps. Frankly, I wish you all were going — but that's not the case. I will read a list of those in barrack 87 who are on the exchange list. Please listen carefully."

Every prisoner there anxiously waited and prayed that his name would be called, including David. Please God, let my name be on the list, he thought. He had not realized that he had actually asked God for a favor.

"Lofland, David," he heard the officer announce, and his knees almost gave way. He quickly recovered enough to listen for his friends' names. He was overjoyed when he heard all three of their names. When the officer left to go to the next building, the four friends jumped up and down and slapped each other on the shoulders.

"Wait," Lum suddenly shouted. "Let's go over round the new mule shed for a minute."

They all knew what Lum was referring to — prayer. There they bowed their heads as Lum thanked the Lord for their release. Lum noticed that David issued the first "Amen."

As the men lay in their bunks that evening, each of the three thought about the Reb prisoners, many in barrack 87, who would not be leaving. Many would die of dysentery, smallpox, hunger, or even by execution. Even in their greatest joy, they felt great sympathy for their colleagues in arms.

The train left the next morning for Washington, D.C. There was much talking and laughing about times in Camp Douglas.

"Know Squirrel didn't eat any of the spaniel. Dogs eat squirrel 'stead of the squirrels eatin' dogs," Lum said, looking at Squirrel and laughing.

"Oh, my gosh, we need to go back," said David in a serious tone.

"Why?" Earl asked, as if worried.

"Forgot to get deloused," David said.

All four men laughed.

"Lum, you think they'd know'd it was you who wrote the poem about the dog — you always doing som'in like that," Squirrel said, again laughing.

"Wish I'd had room for the third verse," Lum said.

"Tell us," begged Earl. "What was the third verse?"

"Well, it related to one day I worked in the mess hall. We's havin' beans — least the Union officers were having beans. The third verse was, "Hee, hee, hee, in your beans is my pee, pee, pee.""

The other three broke out in loud laughter.

"Did you really pee in their beans?" asked David.

"Shor did, 'bout cup full."

The laughter was even louder.

The train got to Washington, D.C. two days later. From the train station, the prisoners would march down to the Potomac River to board ships. The four friends were amazed at the city.

"I never expected to be here right under Lincoln's nose, less'n it was with our Confederate Army," David said, looking over the city as the men marched. "The capitol's bigger than I thought."

"Notice all the Federal soldiers? They ever'where — must be guarding whiskers," Earl observed, referring to Lincoln.

The men marched past an impressive building near an intersection of streets.

"Ford's Theatre," Squirrel read out load. "Must put on plays and singings there — sounds highfalutin to me."

The men finally reached the Potomac River, where two large steam paddle wheelers were docked. The ships would go down the river to the east coast, and then south down the coast to the James River. Under a flag of truce, they would sail up to Center Point, Virginia, just short of the Confederate capital at Richmond. A large number of Union soldiers were already on the ships.

"Be glad to git on the boats, so's these Yankees quit lookin' at us," Lum said, looking down at the ships. "Haven't seen a good-lookin' woman since we got here. All the Yankee women got frowns and hateful looks on their faces."

Around two o'clock, the big ships left the docks on the river. They had to maneuver slowly around seven or eight ironclad gunboats that were stationed at the nation's capital.

April 8 was a warm, spring day, with scattered clouds and a light southern breeze. As the Arkys stood at the ship's railing, they commented about the beautiful Potomac River and the already green countryside of northern Virginia. As the ship passed yet another Federal gunboat proceeding north, Lum eyed it closely as it moved on by the big paddle wheeler.

"Somin's up here in Yankee land, sure as the world. Lot of gunboats at Washington and more coming. Reckon Lee's moving north again, like he did in Maryland?"

"Lemme tell you what I heard when I went to the toilet while ago. I was on the jon and two Yankee officers came in the toilet. They's a'talking while peeing. Didn't know I was in there. One of 'em, a feller with a deep-bass voice, said that General Grant was going to try to take Vicksburg again. Said they's digging a canal around the fort and they wouldn't have to use the Mississippi River. Said he hoped to take it by the first of June," reported Squirrel in a low, hushed voice.

Lum looked down at the shorter soldier.

"Crying out loud. Figured he'd already taken it after McClernerd flushed us outta the Post. They said he had 32,000 men there at Fort Hindman."

David glanced out at another ship, the USS Monroe, as it slowly passed them and continued on toward Washington.

"Those Rebs been hanging on for quite a while at Vicksburg," David said. "If they could get some help, they may defeat General Grunt."

The Chesapeake Bay area was even more beautiful. The ships, about a mile off the Virginia coast, slowly moved south. David thought of springtime in Arkansas. The family was probably preparing to plant early crops. Plowing would be underway. He wondered if Wilburn or William had married. Surely the twins had found a man by then. His mind wandered back to Hickory Flats and Lillie. If only he had been able to read her letter. He was sure that she wanted to tell him that she and the parson had been praying for him.

The troop-laden ships made the turn off the Virginia coast

and up the James River by late afternoon of the second day. After a mile or so, the ship passed another ironclad, but this time it was a Confederate warship. The Reb sailors on the deck of the gunboat, obviously aware of the prisoner exchange at City Point, waved at the prisoners of war.

They passed several nice plantations located along the James River.

"Back in Dixie, men — can feel the difference already," Earl said, scanning the fields along the river. He noticed a Yankee guard looking at him, a distasteful look on his face.

It was nearing dusk and it was becoming more difficult to see along the river. Oney Taylor walked up to the men as they watched the evening light disappear.

"Men, we gonna spend the night aboard the ship," said the adjutant. "Gonna take some time tomorrow to handle the exchange. We'll get off and 300 Federals will git on board. We'll have some paperwork before the release."

The captives were so excited about being released that no one got much sleep aboard the ship on the last night. April 10 in City Point was even more beautiful. The temperature was almost summerlike. By ten o'clock, the long line of Confederate prisoners was moving for the ramp to go ashore.

David also noticed a large number of Federal prisoners in the dock area waiting their turn to board the ship. They were thin and dirty looking, much like the Southerners. As the prisoners filed down the ramp, they noticed a Confederate officer in an immaculate gray uniform giving instructions. Then David's feet touched the hallowed soil of the South. Behind him, Lum dropped to the ground and kissed it.

"Thank you, Lord," David heard him say.

A Confederate officer was there to remind the men to go directly through the door of a large warehouse just off the dock.

After walking to the warehouse and entering a huge room, the men noticed rows of benches. They all stood respectfully until the Confederate officer at the ramp entered the huge room. Three other gray-clad officers followed the first officer, who had moved to an old speaker stand. There he laid down several papers. The officer glanced up, then back to the papers, and up again. He looked over the group before speaking.

"Men, please be seated," he said. "Let me welcome you home. I only wish every man taken as a prisoner was here now. Men, I'm Colonel George Herbert, general staff, Confederate army. You have been paroled, effective today, April 10, 1863. You were exchanged for the Federal prisoners now boarding the ships at the dock. First, we will have you all examined by a physician. If you require medical care, we will see that you get it. "Now," the officer paused, "if you are healthy, you may consider two options. One, you may go home."

Cheers went up all over the facility.

"Secondly, you may also rejoin our Confederate forces who are fighting all over our Southland." The men were quiet when he mentioned that option. "Men, let me introduce Colonel Edwin Washburn, 48th Cavalry, Mississippi."

The prisoners politely applauded as Washburn moved to the podium. The new speaker was tall, with wavy black hair and a well-shaped mustache. Over his left eye was a black patch. As he moved his arms up to grasp the podium, the observers notice that he was missing his left hand. A heavy bandage still covered the shortened arm.

"Men, I ride with Bedford Forrest," he said after clearing his throat.

Bedford Forrest? That name rang a bell with David. Then he remembered the slave auction in Memphis. Forrest owned that auction, along with several plantations. And he had become a general, thought David. Then he remembered that Earl was a cousin of Bedford Forrest.

"We are doing well in the fight, but we are short on powder and ball, horses, shoes, food and clothing, but most of all, we are drastically short on soldiers," the colonel continued speaking. "We are outnumbered in every battle. General Lee is doing a great job here in Virginia, but we need soldiers in the worst way. Knowing the huge sacrifice that you men have already paid, I still would ask you to consider rejoining the Confederate service. Now, you won't have a choice of where to go if you choose to stay with us. The regiments that you belong to are still fighting some place. If you stay, it will have to be with your assigned unit."

He paused again. "Earlier, I told you what we are short on. Now let me tell you what we have much of. Courage. Southern courage. The same courage that enabled us to get our independence the first time from England. And now, the South is fighting for the same reason — independence. The right to form our own type of government."

There was heavy applause and cheers as the colonel hit the motivation button.

"Men of the South — we need you."

Almost every prisoner was on his feet applauding heavily. After the applause ended, the officer spoke again.

"There are two tables behind me. An officer at one table will release you from further duty — and with our many thanks. At the second table you will be reassigned to your old regiment or to the regiment that your original group has been reassigned. May God bless the Confederate States of America."

Almost every soldier that stood up applauding turned to ask someone else what they were going to do. Already men were moving to both tables. Lum looked at his friends who were sitting near him.

"Reckon I'll rejoin."

"Me too," said Earl, looking at the other two.

"I'm a career soldier," said Squirrel as he laughed.

"What the heck; might as well keep you guys straight," said David, glancing around at the other three men.

At the reenlistment table, Earl was told to go to the first table, get his release, and then return for his assignment to the 24th Arkansas. Within three days, the four friends had caught a train in Richmond for Knoxville, Tennessee.

Chapter 30

Reassignment

July 1863

AFTER BEING GRANTED A leave for ten days, the four Arkansans were again healthy and ready to rejoin the Confederate forces. Both Earl and David had recovered sufficiently to resume training and camp exercises.

The Army of Tennessee was camped in eastern Tennessee when the four friends joined the 38th Arkansas, which included what was left of the old 24th Regiment. The four newcomers had hardly settled in before they heard the terrible news.

On July 4, 1863, Vicksburg finally fell to Grant. On the same day, the Union Army under General George Meade turned back Robert E. Lee's Army of Northern Virginia. The South suffered a double blow — one in the North and one in the South. No major activity occurred in east Tennessee during the fall of 1863 except for an occasional raid by General Forrest.

They heard of the terrible draft riots in New York City only a few days later. More than 50,000 people broke into the New York draft office and burned it, nearly killing the superintendent. More than 1,000 people were killed or wounded.

"The Northern folks gittin' tired of the war when they turn on each other," David said when he heard the story.

"Reckon Lincoln will pull off us?" Earl asked, as the men sat around the open fire.

"Doubt it," Lum replied. "Especially after they have finally won a couple of battles."

Squirrel had opened a letter from home and had not been listening to the conversation.

"Oh no," he now said, as David tossed another piece of wood on the fire.

The other three Rebs looked over at Squirrel, expecting him to tell of a tragedy that had occurred in his family in Nola.

"What is it?" Lum asked in a concerned tone.

"Glenda got married — one of the Stump boys from over Shelton Mountain," he said, still reading the letter.

"I would think you would be glad for big G," Earl said, smiling.

"What's Stump do for a living?" asked Lum.

"Question is, what he's ever done? His shovel handle is only half there," Squirrel answered, not smiling.

The three friends all laughed.

"I'm really hurt, Squirrel. I have been waiting for my love all this time and I get jilted by this Stump feller. Clean shot out of the saddle," Lum related as the others laughed.

"Must be a right smart, good-looking lad to replace me," Lum said, grinning at Squirrel.

"Ole boy going on 300 pounds — that's 'fore dinner too," Squirrel answered.

"Shor was looking forward to being your brother'n–law, Squirrel," Lum said, again looking at the small Reb.

"Don't fret, Lum. Still got 'nother that's looking," Squirrel said, looking back at Lum.

"Well, Stump married a good cook, anyway," Earl said as the other three continued to joke about Squirrel's sister.

"Yeah, she'll be up half the night cooking for — what was his first name?" asked David, grinning at the others.

"Don't really know. I always called him rotten. Rotten Stump — my new brother'n-law."

David also received his first letter from home, after informing his family of his whereabouts. They were delighted and praised the Lord for his release from the prison camp in Chicago. However, from David's end, there was more bad news. Uncle Seth and Aunt Allie had both died from a serious epidemic of scarlet fever. Even worse, Becky had died in childbirth shortly after he left, and the baby died three days later. All four relatives were buried at the Young Gravelly Cemetery.

Wilburn had married his lady friend, Grace Mason, and they now lived in Seth and Allie's home. William was courting a new lady in church and Junior had finally interested Melonie Hall in a relationship. His ma was doing reasonable well, although she had some problems with her balance and movement. Rachel seemed to be taking care of his ma.

David was saddened to hear that he had lost his aunt and uncle. They were so loving and helpful. No doubt, they had worked awfully hard to help build the new Lofland home and help the family get a new start in Arkansas. However, he was shocked beyond belief about losing the twin — and her baby. It seemed that nothing good happened lately to the Lofland family. He wished that he could see his ma. He wished that he had told her more often how much he loved her. But he also missed his whole family. Rather than wait, David got paper from the adjutant and wrote a long letter to his family in Bluffton.

~~~

Desertion had become a serious problem for the Southern

army. Adjutant Taylor reported that the desertion rates were up to 20 percent, and it was not expected to improve.

Joe Johnston's Confederate army, growing smaller by the day, now faced its most serious problem. When Lincoln called Grant back east to confront the wirily Robert E. Lee, General William Sherman, who had led Union troops at Fort Hindman and again at Vicksburg, replaced Grant.

Sherman was now assigned the task of winning the war in the eastern Mississippi Valley. The stubborn general had developed a new idea in modern warfare: to defeat the stubborn South by destroying their means of making a living — total war. With a vast, modern-equipped army, Sherman would abandon his army's lifeline, the Mississippi River, and strike out across the South and either destroy or confiscate all Southern resources for his vast army.

Mississippi and Alabama would soon feel the ravages of the Union army. The army would burn homes and buildings and confiscate or destroy crops. They would slay farm animals for food. They would destroy towns and railroads. They would kill citizens and slaves.

Displeased at Joe Johnston's effort to stop the Union machine, President Davis would replace him with another Rebel hero, John Bell Hood. The new general, who had taken a lot of criticism for the failure at Gettysburg, would try to prove himself, once given the command that he desired.

The change in Confederate command would not affect the 38th Arkansas Regiment. The four friends, with somewhat better food now, were healthy enough to march and fight. They had also received additional training in Tennessee.

"They sent us down to stop that Sherman feller. Only ones he's been fighting is farmers. See how he does with some Camp Douglas-hardened Rebs," Lum said as the men sat around the fire.

"Got our secret weapon — Super Squirrel. He'll burrow under their feathers. If that don't work, we'll sic the world's champion mule rider on them. Saddle up, Blue."

The men laughed.

"Course, we still got Earl the girl," Lum said, smiling.

"Ho-hum, Lum, will be in reserve," said Lum, still grinning.

"Lum, if you ever get shot in the head, hope they look inside. I'd like to see what's in there," Earl said as they all laughed.

David looked around the fire at the other three men.

"Least we down here in the South where there's good looking women — 'member those Washington maids?"

"Member that chubby midget woman? You see Squirrel eyeing her?" joked Lum.

"If those two hooked up, their young'un wouldn't be over a foot high."

Again the men laughed as Lum looked over at Squirrel.

"You better not be looking 'round for women, Lum. I wrote my other sister, Mavis, 'bout you — and proposed for you. Said I would be best man at the wedding," Squirrel said, looking at Lum without smiling. "She's the real looker in the family. She'd hog dress out less than 250. Only thing is keeping her single. Reckon you'll be all right less'n another Stump boy shows up."

The men all laughed. Lum, who usually led all conversations, looked around at the man again.

"Guess it's bedtime; care if I pray?" There were a couple of no's.

"Gotta go to the latrine," David said, getting up. The others bowed as their leader led in a prayer.

The next morning, as the four friends ate the normal breakfast of hardtack, Captain Robinson rode up to the camp on his beautiful, grey horse. The men could see that he had a serious look on his face. Several of the other campers moved over to hear the officer's instructions. The captain cleared his throat and began to speak.

"Men, we are pulling up camp and leaving. Gonna be a long march — maybe a week or so. All I can say now, except be ready to move out by noon."

The officer wheeled his horse to the right and moved over to another group of soldiers, where he repeated his instructions.

By 1:00 p.m., the small Rebel army, minus some 200 more deserters, began to march south to southern Tennessee. None of the officers would give out any information as to where the army was headed. As the soldiers moved into a southerly direction in long, double lines, David looked at Lum, who was marching beside him.

"We retreating or going to another battle site?"

"Who knows — but as quickly as we pulled out, you'd think we were retreating," Lum answered, looking toward the head of the column.

Chapter 31

Battle

September 1863

BY MID–SEPTEMBER, THE ARMY was camped near a small creek in northwestern Georgia. The locals referred to the creek as Chickamauga, obviously an old Indian name. Within days, the Reb army, now under General Bragg, was preparing to meet a huge Union army under a General Rosecrans.

In the worst fighting of the war, more than 2,000 Rebs were killed and more than 14,000 wounded. The Federals lost more than 1,600 men, with almost 10,000 wounded. Both sides lost almost 28 percent of their strength in the Battle of Chickamauga. Yet, the Confederates could finally claim a victory. Once again, Lum led a prayer of thanksgiving for the safety of the four friends.

By November, the Rebel army had marched further north, not far from a Tennessee town called Chattanooga. Camp was established and pickets put in place. From the anxiety on the faces of the officers, it was apparent to the foot soldiers that a battle was expected soon.

"I keep hearing again about this Sherman general — guess we gonna fight his army," Earl said as he finished cleaning his musket.

"Ya'll, get your ammo ration — forty rounds, they said, won't last long if it is another Chickamauga," Squirrel said, watching Earl clean his gun.

The four friends, sitting on the ground, looked up to see Lieutenant Nigh moving toward them.

"Men, the 38th and the 21st Regiment will be held in reserve," the officer spoke. "When the rest of the army marches out, you are to stay here — but prepare to move as needed. Have your haversacks packed and ready."

The officer walked on toward other members of the 38th Regiment camped nearby.

"Reckon the Lord is watching over us," Lum said, looking around at his friends.

The Battle of Chattanooga proved to be a disaster for the Southerners. Since the reserve units, including the 38th Regiment, were never summoned, the four friends never saw action against the touted William Sherman.

"How you gonna defeat the Yanks without the "fearless foursome?" Lum asked as the dilapidated Rebel army marched south again into Georgia.

"We gonna be in Atlanta 'fore long," Squirrel surmised.

"Well, least there's good-looking women there," Lum said as the march continued.

"Somebody hang on to Squirrel when we get to Atlanta," David said. "He said he had growed an inch since Camp Douglas. He's going to be looking for long, tall women now."

The other men, including Squirrel, laughed.

"Oh, those Georgia peaches," Earl sang in a made-up song.

"Shut up, Earl. You're even scaring the crows away with your terrible voice," Lum said as he laughed.

"Ya'll notice that the weather is already cooling down. Could be a bad winter," David said.

"But, Blue, probably won't be much fighting in the winter
— especially if it is a bad winter with snow," Lum answered.

Chapter 32

Winter

December/January, 1863-64

THE WINTER OF 1863 was one of the coldest winters in history. By mid–December, temperatures were below zero in most of the North and even part of the South. Snow, seldom seen in Georgia, occurred on a regular basis. Although not deep, the snow presented its own problems.

Several men came down sick with pneumonia and other diseases in December. Four members of the 38th Regiment perished. Frostbite was a problem; most of the soldiers tied old rags around their hands, hoping to avoid it and the possible loss of fingers. With little or no food, three horses from the artillery corps also died. Now the enemy was the severe winter, which contributed to disease and the lack of food for both men and animals.

To prepare their winter quarters, the four friends spent almost a week constructing an underground bunker. They dug a large hole about four feet deep and then covered it with old logs and brush. Part of an old barn door served as the door for the homemade cellar. Once they had completed the job, the men opened the crude door and went down the three steps, where they had to duck to get under the low roof.

"You guys ever thought about it — we have dug holes at Fort Hindman and helped with the tunnel at Camp Douglas," David said, glancing around the structure.

"Blue, I never thought we'd build a White Oak after staying in the Camp Douglas dungeon," Lum said, looking over at David.

"You gotta admit the Yankee's dungeon was a little tighter than ours," retorted Squirrel. "Can see daylight through our roof."

"Yeah, but at least we can git out to pee and crap," Earl replied.

"Lum, we not going to have to sing in here again, are we?" Squirrel asked, "Cause Earl sings like a squawking crow. Listening to him in the White Oak made me want to raise that heavy dungeon door and run."

The others laughed.

"But, you know, that Reuben could really sing," Lum said, thinking about the now deceased soldier that shared the stay in White Oak.

"We better git out and finish our work. We need to build a drainage ditch around the bunker or it will fill with water during a heavy rain," David suggested to his friends.

The cold, northern wind was blowing harder and dark clouds hurried across the sky. Snow could be on the way, David thought as he brought additional cedar tree limbs to put on the roof of the bunker. He glanced over to the right, where Bob Hatfield, George Meyers, and "Cap" Williams were working on a similar bunker. By then, the three soldiers were shoveling dirt on top of their cellar.

"Hey, you guys going to bed down with snakes. They will enjoy your cozy home," David offered.

"Naw, we gonna borrow Squirrel to chase them off," replied Hatfield.

As David glanced back to his three other friends, he noticed Earl taking the big bandage off his left arm. He had been slightly wounded at Chickamauga when he took a mini–ball in the arm.

"Not infected, is it?" David asked, looking at the wounded arm.

"Don't thank so — but they's some pus," he said, again wrapping the dirty bandage around the arm.

~~~

January was even colder. Any water left out would quickly freeze. While the men now wore two suits of clothing, Lum worried about possible frostbite.

With no military action, the soldiers now mainly tried to stay warm and secure food. By 1864, the Confederate government in Richmond had serious financial problems. The most pressing problem was funding the war, which had been going on four years. Loans from European powers were no longer possible. Providing food for the Confederate army was nearly impossible.

President Davis was forced to find some solution to the problem. The chief executive issued stern orders that only created more hardships on the struggling Southern population. In Virginia, Davis authorized General Lee to commandeer food supplies from the local population. Even though a necessity, the orders did not improve his popularity.

Forage patrols were established. All kinds of livestock, including horses, could be commandeered. The Virginia people, with an ongoing battleground in their midst, had already been hiding livestock from the Federal army, which had lifted much of the agricultural produce for their own use.

"The captain said we's on forage patrol tomorrow," Lum announced to his friends as he climbed back into the bunker after going to the latrine. "And man, is it cold out there. I'm going up to build a fire. Then we will have squirrel for dinner."

There was some laughter. After Lum left, the other three men crawled over to the doorway. David raised the makeshift door and looked outside. There was at least four inches of snow on the ground and more coming down. The men exited the bunker and began to move out away from the area to search for firewood. They noticed several other Reb soldiers out looking for firewood.

While David looked over the snow-covered ground, he thought about Lum's prayer the night before. He actually thanked God for their situation. Only hell could be worse than this. What kind of thinking was that?

As he looked out in the distance for any sign of something that would burn, his foot hit a rock that was covered with snow. Plunging forward into the snow, he quickly reached out his hands to break the fall. When he hit the frozen turf, his left arm turned inside toward his body. He felt a sharp pain in his forearm and knew that it had to be broken. David painfully picked himself up off the snow-covered ground. Holding his left arm carefully with his right hand, he started back to the captain's tent to report the incident.

The medic, though not a doctor, determined that David's arm was broken. Thirty minutes later, with a homemade splint and a sling for his arm, David got back to the bunker. By then a fire was burning and a small stack of wood was close by. When they saw David, his three friends quickly stood up.

"What happened?" asked Earl, as they all looked at David.

"Oh, clumsy as usual — fell over a rock and broke my arm. Harris, the medic, put it into a sling."

"Blue, you would do anything to get out of the forage patrol tomorrow," stated Lum, examining the splinted arm and laughing.

The fire seemed to break the icy chill. As the men crowded around close to it, there was little conversation. They had eaten some horsemeat the day before, but now they had no food left, and each man was thinking about a warm meal — preferably home-cooked. David was thinking about his ma's breakfast. She often had biscuits, gravy, eggs and grits. Gosh, her red-eyed gravy was good. Would he ever taste it again?

An officer rode up as the men stared into the enchanting fire.

"'Low, Captain," Lum said, looking at the man and his boney horse.

"Ya'll ready to go on forage patrol?" the captain asked, looking at the fire.

"Well, we all ready 'cept Blue; he broke an arm not over an hour ago," Lum replied, nodding toward David.

"Sorry, but I need you other three men for the detail. Horses back at the persimmon grove — need to be there in ten minutes," he said as he quickly turned his horse back toward the grove.

The three friends took a moment to console David for breaking his arm and not being able to go on the patrol. Then they left, moving back in the direction of the persimmon grove.

The three mules, all confiscated from the artillery corps, were as bad or worse than the captain's horse. Lum wondered if his mule would even support him, as poorly as it looked.

With the captain leading, the three friends left in an easterly direction on horseback. There was little or no conversation among the men as they moved behind the captain in single file. After riding over an hour, the patrol topped a tree-covered hill and looked down into a long valley below. There, along a frozen creek, was a small cabin. Smoke was coming from the chimney. They could see a small log barn, chicken house, and outhouse behind the cabin.

"Let's check it out, men," commanded the officer.

The four riders slowly descended the hill on their mounts. As they neared the floor of the valley, Lum noticed a man coming from the barn with a bucket. He wondered if he had just finished milking. The captain led the patrol up to the back door of the old cabin.

"Keep your guns ready, men," the officer suggested. "They sometimes defend their property."

As the captain dismounted, the old man they had seen opened the back door.

"Howdy," he said to the men. "Ya'll like to come in out of the cold?"

"Would it be all right?" the captain replied in a surprised manner.

"Shore," he said.

By then, the dismounted men noticed an old woman who had come to the door by her husband.

"Know you'uns are Rebs, 'cause you look hungry," she said, looking around at the foursome.

As the old man opened the door for the men, each could smell bacon cooking.

"Ya'll have a seat while I put more bacon and eggs on the fire," she said, turning to go toward a large, wood-burning stove as the old man stepped outside to bring in more firewood. Squirrel noticed that the cabin was quite warm, probably due to both the kitchen stove and the burning fireplace.

The breakfast was delicious.

"Ma'am, you do breakfast right," complimented Earl,

finishing off a biscuit. "Shame Blue's not here."

"Thank you," the old woman responded.

Now that the breakfast was over, it was time for the captain's explanation for the visit. None of the other men would have liked to take his place.

"We were sent out on a forage patrol — find food for our army. We are near starving. As much as I hate, we must take food back to our men. Do you have a cow?" he asked, studying the old man.

"Yow, got a good Jersey cow — she give 'bout gallon of milk, though she's kind of poor now."

"Any hogs or chickens?" the captain asked.

"Check the barn and see for yourself, men; we don't have much, but we's willing to share," he said, looking over at his wife.

The captain stood up and looked at the other three soldiers.

"Search the outbuildings for livestock. Also, look for corn. Our animals need food too."

With Lum leading, the three friends exited the back door and moved toward the outbuildings.

"Earl, you and Squirrel search the barn and hayloft, and I will go to the chicken house," Lum said, moving in that direction.

Once he had reached it, he opened the door and looked inside. He saw four chickens and a turkey. He paused, stepped back and closed the door. Then he heard a shot from the barn. With his gun ready, Lum carefully moved toward the barn.

Once there, he cautiously opened the door. He heard a voice in the far corner of the barn. It belonged to Earl. Lum slowly moved back to the corner of the barn, where Earl was dragging something out of a small pen. It was a pig that he had shot. When they heard someone approaching, Earl and Squirrel whirled around, both with guns in position.

"Lum, come here," Earl requested, recognizing their friend. "We finally found one hog. You don't see any more in the pen, do you?"

Lum looked over into the hog pen, where he saw two more pigs.

"Naw, don't see anymore. Ya'll did a good job," he said, smiling at Earl.

"Have any chickens?" Squirrel asked.

"Not a nary one," he said, holding up four fingers.

Earl tied a rope onto the cow and led her from the barn. By then, the captain had come out to check for any foodstuffs.

"Well, got us a cow and a pig; that will help a lot. Sorry folks, but I'm only following orders," he said, glancing back toward the old couple.

"Take care," the old man responded.

Neither the old man nor the old woman noticed the smiles on the faces of the last three men that followed the captain.

~~~

Although many died during the terrible winter, mostly of disease, the strongest survived. However, many of the strongest decided to desert.

March was not a month for moving armies and military campaigns. Except for the heroics of General Nathan Bedford Forrest, there was little joy in the Rebel camps.

By May, skirmishing had broken out between William Sherman's Federal forces and Joe Johnston's Rebel troops near Stone Church, Georgia. The 38th Regiment, marching forty miles in two days, arrived east of Stone Church not long after the small battle. Only eight Rebs had been killed. However, fourteen Federals had paid the price. In a few days Johnston's combined army, now at 62,000, began a cautious march toward another small Georgia town, Dalton.

David's arm now healed. After the kidding that he had taken from his three friends, he was determined not to miss any more action.

Once Johnston's army made camp near Dalton, the major activity was scouting for and preparing for Sherman's 100,000–man army, which was moving from Tennessee.

In late June, the Arky boys were sitting around the campfire after eating a good meal consisting of beans and cornbread. Food was more plentiful in Georgia than in Tennessee.

"Captain said General Early almost captured Washington D.C. — can you believe that? And yet, Grant is on the doorstep of our capital at Richmond," Earl said, looking into the fire.

"We win some, but lose more," David said. "Grunt may take Richmond, but he will have to take Lee," Lum offered.

"Squirrel, you not saying much tonight; you thinking about a girlfriend?" David asked, smiling at the smaller soldier.

"Hey, I'm tired after digging all day on those fortification ditches. This is the fifth straight day of digging ditches. I've got blisters all over. Can hardly hold a fork."

"After Fort Hindman, we ought to be good at building gun pits," David said as he stood up to prepare for bed.

Chapter 33

Dalton, Georgia

July 1864

IT WAS ANOTHER BRIGHT, sunny day in the south. There was a breeze, with some gusts of wind. In the rear, hospital wagons had moved forward not far from the munitions wagons. Everyone had consumed the ordinary breakfast — hardtack, with most complaining. With everything ready for a possible Union attack, the soldiers had been allowed to sit down on the new piles of dirt and visit. Tobacco was evident, in both the chewing and the smoking variety. One foursome from the 38th Regiment was playing cards. Surprisingly, the atmosphere was mainly relaxed.

As David and his friends sat looking out in the direction of a possible enemy approach, they saw a rider quickly approaching from the north. He rode up to an officer who had stepped out to meet him. They could see the two men talking and gesturing. Then the rider shook his head, saluted, and wheeled his horse to go back in the direction that he had come. The officer walked over to a bugler and he soon responded with the alert signal — and repeated it again. Down the line, other buglers passed the signal on.

The four Arkys slowly got up, while looking towards the

north. In the far distance, they could hear enemy bugles sounding. One of the lieutenants in the 38th Regiment was making his way down the back side of the long trench, reminding the men to check cartridges and guns and to make sure their canteens were filled with water.

David glanced back south. The artillery corps was making last-minute preparations. The 38th Regiment, as part of Hardee's corps, was ready. The men stood outside the ditches and strained their eyes to see any activity in the distant north.

"They are coming!" someone down to the west shouted.

The blue-clads came into view. It was an almost perfect line. They could see the colorful battle flags and the Union officers out front on horseback. David swallowed. There must be 20,000 of them, all ready to die to subjugate the South, he though.

It suddenly sounded like the earth exploded, as the Southern artillery released their terrible salvos. Their first shells were short. Maybe this was why the Federals had not fired their big guns, thought David. In a couple of minutes, the Federal cannon began to mimic the sounds of the Rebel cannon. David saw that some of the Union shells were short of their target. Others were certainly long, he knew, because one shell hit a loaded munitions wagon back behind them. He wondered how many Rebs were killed as a result of that shot.

David heard the screams of wounded and dying Southerners in between the Yankee cannon sounds. Then he had a strange thought: man was truly a hatemonger. He had elevated the killing of his fellow man to a science. The only question was which — the blue-clads or the gray-clads — would do the best job that day?

It had been a beautiful day when it started. Now, the haze in the air created by the exploding gunpowder and the dust and debris had erased the day that had been intended for mankind. A Federal shell landed in the creek, twenty feet or so in front of them, with a loud thump. Creek water sprayed over everyone in that area.

David glanced to his right, as another soldier had dropped into the trench between he and Lum. He quickly looked back toward the now stationary Union line of soldiers, and then looked back again to the stranger.

"Howdy," David said, briefly studied the soldier. A thin, dark-haired man, he had black eyes and a short goatee.

"Mornin'," came a response from the thin lips.

With a lull in the activity out front, David glanced again toward the stranger.

"Where ya from?"

"Pine Bluff, Arkansas — 'bout you?" responded the man, continuing to gaze out toward the Union army. "

"An Arky too. Been in long?" David asked, noticing that the terrific shelling had almost stopped.

"'Bout year, I reckon, and I hate it. Been in the guardhouse most of the time. "Wished I's there now," the man said, turning and spitting behind the ditch.

"Why'd you join up?" David's curiosity prompted him to ask.

"Aw, got in some trouble back in Pine Bluff. Joined up to 'void the law," the man said, finally glancing at David.

"What'd you do?" David asked, again wondering why the activity out front had slowed down.

"Aw, got involved with some guys who were robbing folks, mostly travelers — lot of 'em squatter trash. We'd steal their goods and sell them. One of the guys was a storeowner there in north Pine Bluff. Nothing real bad — making good money. Then one evening, we went out to check on this ole boy who had come by the store with a load of furniture on his wagon —

pulled by oxen. I thought the other two just meant to rob him — oh, maybe rough him up a little. I'd never killed anybody 'afore. One of 'em cut his throat — couldn't believe it. Law caught both of 'em — hung 'em. I's on the run fer while till I joined the army."

After a pause, David glanced back at the man.

"You have a family?"

"Did one time — three screaming young'uns and an ole lady that didn't like my drinking and gambling. Forced to knock 'em around a lot. Had all I could take and left 'em about six year ago."

David stared at the man for several seconds. Suddenly the bugles sounded. He could hear the Rebel officers shouting as they moved up and down the fortified trench. They were going to leave the safety of the big trench, David realized. They were going to charge the blue-clad invaders.

"Let's go, men. We gonna charge 'em," an officer shouted.

The bugles sounded again. The Southerners climbed out of the ditch and crossed Peachtree Creek with a loud Rebel cheer. They quickly re-formed in a line and began to advance toward the Union army that had begun to advance again. Musket fire began on both sides, as the different colored lines moved toward each other.

David could not see Lum, Earl, or Squirrel. He hoped they were okay. After firing his musket at least three times, and with Rebs falling all around him, David met the first Federal soldier in hand-to-hand combat. As he threw up his gun to ward off the Yank's bayonet thrust, he thought, I will die before I let you Yankees take me prisoner again.

David's bayonet thrust was also pushed aside as the two men struggled to save their lives. As the Yank thrust his bayonet at David's throat, he ducked and the blade went over his head. He quickly thrust his own bayonet at the man's stomach. He felt the knife penetrate the soldier's flesh, as the man fell backward. He hit the ground on his back and the bayonet buried into the dirt under his body.

David looked to his right, where a Federal soldier had Squirrel on the ground. He screamed and the Yank turned quickly to face him. As he brought his gun back to prepare a thrust of his bayonet, Squirrel's hunting knife plunged into the soldier's body below the rib cage. David suddenly felt a blow to the head. He fell to the ground from the force of the man's gun butt. The soldier recoiled for a thrust at the helpless Reb on the ground. David quickly rolled and the Union bayonet sank into the dirt about three inches from his body. The soldier screamed, and David knew someone had shot him.

David confronted several other Federals, most whom would not survive, before the Yankees sounded retreat. As the blue-clads fell back, David looked around. He saw bodies all around on the ground — some dressed in blue, some in gray, and many more dressed as average, Southern farmers. Most of the Rebs left standing were in a daze.

None of the exhausted Rebs noticed David go over to a dark-haired Reb — one with a short goatee — who was lying on the ground dead. David silently reached down and pulled the hunting knife from the dead soldier's back. He glanced down at the soldier once more, wiped the hunting knife on his pant leg, and slipped it back into its sheath in his belt.

Slightly dazed himself, he turned and began to look for his friends. Then off to his left he saw Earl, a heavy bandage on his left arm, being supported by Squirrel. Both were dirty and tired looking, but both managed a brief smile.

"What about Lum? Ya'll see him?" David asked in a concerned manner.

Earl's smile turned to a frown. "He was hit by shell or shrapnel. Upper thigh — looked bad. They took him back toward Atlanta to the hospital."

Suddenly, they heard cannon fire again from the north.

"Get back to the trench," screamed an officer.

Shells were falling over the area even before the men could get back to the big ditch. The Federal cannon fire grew worse, but David could hardly hear the sporadic Rebel cannon fire. The Arkys had made it to the bottom of the ditch when the fire seemed to become more intense.

Oh, God, help us, thought David. It sounded like the enemy shells were hitting all around them. Even with the devastating artillery explosions, he could hear screams from Reb soldiers.

"Oh God, this is hell," muttered David, looking up at the smoke and dust-filled sky.

The Union continued their artillery assault for more than two hours. When the cannon fire lessened, David wondered if the Union infantry was advancing. He turned and rose up to look back north. Then he screamed as a projectile of some kind hit him below the right shoulder. He glimpsed a large amount of his own blood as he staggered and fell unconscious to the bottom of the ditch. Earl and Squirrel screamed for a medic, but he didn't hear them.

Chapter 34

Hospital

HE AWOKE — WAS IT heaven? It looked like a blue sky. But then he realized it was a room — a hospital room with a blue ceiling. He started to turn his head to look to his right. Oh, it hurt terribly. He was beginning to remember. He had been wounded. But where were Earl, Squirrel, and Lum? Then he vaguely remembered hearing that Lum had been seriously wounded. A nurse — a woman — was coming to check on him. Then he remembered: this was Atlanta — a big city with real hospitals. They had female nurses.

"How you feeling?" the older woman said as she adjusted his pillow.

"Guess all right, but my shoulder really hurts," David replied, trying to look down at the wound.

"Your nickname Blue?" the nurse asked.

"Guess so," he replied.

"You had visitors earlier. A man 'bout your size and a little short feller," the lady said, handing David a cup of water.

"Probably Earl and Squirrel."

"Well, one's name was Earl," she said, reaching up to feel his face. "No temperature; that's good. Oh, by the way, there's a fellow in the next ward from the 38th Regiment. Thought you might know him," she said, smiling. "Name's Lumry; know him by chance?"

"That's Lum! He's okay? Thank the Lord."

"Well, he's not in very good shape; they had to remove his left leg. Hurt bad, but he is conscious some of the time."

"Ma'am, is there any way I might be moved in there by Lum?" David pleaded, looking up at the woman.

"Not supposed to, but let me get someone to help me," she said after a brief pause.

She left but soon returned with a male nurse. Together they rolled his bed through a large double door and then about halfway down through the next room. An empty bed had been pulled out to make room for David's. As they rolled the bed into the vacant spot, David tried to look over at his wounded friend, but it hurt to move.

They placed the head of the bed against the wall, and then the female nurse brought a second pillow over to put under David's head. His head was now elevated enough that he could see his friend to his left. Lum was sleeping.

At about 11:30 a.m., the male nurse brought David some hot soup. Once he had finished the soup, he fell asleep again. That evening, David awoke to a lot of pain and to find a doctor by Lum's bed. The doctor was quietly talking to Lum. As the doctor walked away, David looked over at his friend, who was now staring at the blue ceiling.

"Any geese up there anywhere?" asked David, watching his friend.

"I'd recognize that voice anyplace," Lum replied softly as he slowly turned his head toward David. "How long you been here, Blue?"

"Close to a day; how you feeling?" asked David, straining his neck to look at Lum.

"Blue, I was just thinking 'bout you. Well, all of us, when

we's in the White Oak — 'member?" Lum said, trying to see David's face. "Don't know how we made it, especially the smallpox. They'as dying like flies."

"You in lotta pain, Lum?" David asked, changing the subject.

"Quite a bit, I guess. How 'bout you, Blue?"

"Some, but not much as you, I'm sure," David said.

"Yeah, had to take off my leg, but I've stood on one leg before," he joked.

David thought, he still has a good sense of humor. They talked awhile longer before Lum gradually drifted off to sleep. David wondered about Squirrel and Earl and how the war was going.

That evening after supper, David drifted off into his own troubled sleep. It seemed like he dreamed for much of the night. In his dream, he had died. After his death, he was some place, but he didn't know where. In the dream he saw his pa.

"No, David, you were a believer!" he kept yelling at him. "You were a believer!"

He suddenly woke up. His neck and face were wet from a cold sweat. He was afraid. After lying there for more than an hour, he went back to sleep. When he woke up the next morning, he recalled the terrible dream — probably the worst dream that he ever had. He wanted to tell Lum about it.

A doctor came by after breakfast and examined David's shoulder.

"Seems to be doing pretty good; 'nother week, you may be able to leave."

That was positive news. The doctor turned around to take a look at Lum. The middle-aged nurse had also come to Lum's bedside.

"He's got a fever — not good. Started putting cold washrags on his forehead — need to break that fever."

Lum opened his eyes just before the doctor and nurse left.

"Guy can't get any rest around here anymore," he joked in a whisper.

"You not ready for battle yet, young man," the doctor said, feeling Lum's arms. Then he followed the nurse out the door.

"Blue, you snored last night like one of those Yankee trains," Lum joked, looking over at David.

David laughed and then paused.

"Lum, I had a bad dream last night," he told his friend. "Got me kinda worried."

"Okay, spit it out partner. What happened?" Lum asked in a strong whisper.

David told his friend what he had dreamed. Still not able to look directly at his friend, Lum listened carefully. David finished his story about the dream the night before.

"What do you think, Lum? What's it mean?"

His buddy cleared his throat.

"Blue, you are my best friend." Lum began in a hoarse whisper. David already felt a tear welling up in one of his eyes. "If ya believe that, then please hear me out. I've been with ya for 'bout a year. I heard what ya said about your faith when we's in the White Oak. You got some serious doubts about God — and Jesus Christ. You've told about why ya have doubts. And, Blue, ya have gone through more than most at your age. But, Blue, when God created mankind, he didn't create a puppet that he could control by pulling on strings to do what he wanted. He wanted a being that would have choices — one that on his own could choose between right and wrong. Choice was one of the main things that God gave us."

Lum coughed twice.

"So, man often chooses to do evil, rather than good. You've made the wrong choices yourself, as we all have. Blue, God didn't make those darkie slaves — man, did. God didn't mistreat the Indians on the Trail of Tears. And God didn't cause your pa to be murdered. Evil men made a choice to kill your pa."

David immediately thought about his actions on the battlefield earlier with the Pine Bluff man who had helped murder his pa. It had been his choice.

Lum coughed again.

"Now, Blue, 'bout your girlfriend, Lillie. God had nothing to do with her marriage to the preacher. The preacher was probably really looking for a new mate. You know Lillie's parents really wanted the best for their daughter — a Christian man with a home and a few possessions. All parents want that. Unfortunately, her parents seemed to forget that God gave us a choice and they overlooked Lillie's choice in the matter. You've been tough on preachers and there are some bad ones, even in the Bible."

Lum coughed again. His voice was getting weaker.

"You've told about the preacher who was raping the young, black, female slave, and how the girl's enslaved brother murdered the evil preacher. Blue, the preacher had ignored God. He chose evil over good. God allows all of us to go our own way — and sometimes we match the devil himself."

If Lum could've seen his best friend, he would have noticed the tears in David's blue eyes.

"But, Blue, God does bless us — sometimes even after we make a lot of wrong choices."

The cough was longer this time.

"How have you been blessed? Let me remind ya, Blue. You have survived Fort Hindman, then Camp Douglas with the White Oak, scurvy, Morgan's Mule, rotten food, and smallpox, where hundreds died. Of all the soldiers at Camp Douglas, we were released in a prisoner exchange. And now, you have survived the battle of Dalton, Georgia."

David found himself listening carefully. Almost 2,200 Rebs had paid the ultimate price at Peachtree Creek. For some reason, he hadn't been one of them.

"Blue, how else can God bless you?" Lum said. "Thousands have died in our losing cause. Chances are, Sherman will take Atlanta and all of Georgia 'fore long and we may have to surrender — but in the worst possible tragedy, God is still there."

Lum had to pause. He thought he could hear David crying, although silently.

"Lum — I, I, I'm sorry. I understand much better now. Thanks for talking with me," David answered, almost breaking down crying.

"Look, Blue. I love ya as my Christian brother, and if something happens, I will want ya in heaven with me someday."

"I love you too, Lum," David answered in a soft, shaky voice.

"Good. Now hush and let me get some rest," he said as he laughed softly.

~~~

Lum never woke up after the conversation with David. The cause of death was pneumonia. The shock was almost unbearable for David. He lay in the bed and cried for hours about the loss of his friend.

And then he prayed and prayed. He apologized to God, and then he thanked God for allowing him to have such a perceptive Christian friend as Lum. No doubt, Lum himself had been a blessing from God.

Chapter 35

Release

August 1864

FOUR DAYS LATER, DAVID was sitting in the waiting area of the hospital. He had learned the day before that Squirrel and Earl were east of Atlanta with the Confederate army. An officer had also informed him that he was being released from further military duty and he could go home to Arkansas. As he sat waiting to sign the release papers, David hardly noticed the two nurses that came out of one office and went into an adjacent office.

"Mr. Lofland — your next," a nurse called out. As he moved over to the office window, David glanced at the other men waiting for a release from the hospital.

"Feeling okay?" the nurse asked as she handed him the necessary papers to sign.

"Better than a long time," David replied, signing the papers.

"Well, good luck," the nurse said, preparing to call the next man.

"Thanks," he said.

As he turned to walk toward the door of the hospital and leave, someone shouted his name. He turned to see a tall, slender woman in a white nurse's uniform. Long, blonde hair touched her shoulders. The attractive woman had a bewildering but beautiful smile on her face. Suddenly, he realized — it was Lillie.

They both ran toward the middle of the waiting room, where they tightly and openly embraced each other in front of everyone present. He looked down at her. She was even more beautiful. The lucky parson, he thought.

"David, I can't believe it. Let's step in the office over there," she said, hanging tightly onto his arm. Once in the other room, she turned to him.

"David, did you get my letter?" she asked, looking into his eyes.

"It got there, but a Yankee officer destroyed it before I could read it," he replied. He still could not believe he was talking to her.

"Oh, you never got to read it?" Lillie asked with a slight frown.

"No, but I attacked the Union officer for not letting me have it," he said, looking back into her beautiful green eyes.

"David, Bud died of smallpox about three months after you all moved to Arkansas," she said in a soft voice. "By then, I thought that you probably had another girl or even a wife. Later, I finally got enough nerve to write your parents in Bluffton. It must've taken two months for them to get the letter. They wrote back that 4,700 Southern prisoners of war had been captured at Fort Hindman, and since they had received no notice, they assumed that you were in the prisoner group taken north. Later, the newspapers reported that some of the prisoners of war were dropped at Camp Butler in Springfield and some were taken on to Chicago to Camp Douglas. I wrote to Camp Butler and they reported that you were never there. I then decided to try to reach you at Camp Douglas. I have been so worried that something had happened to you there since I never got a letter back. David, I have just prayed and prayed for you."

Now there were tears in both of their eyes. Lillie had pulled David closer.

"But, Lillie, how did you get here in Atlanta? David asked, a puzzled look on his face. "You had no idea that I would be here."

"Father has a brother here in Atlanta," Lillie said, looking down and then back at David. "After my husband's funeral, Uncle Dennis wrote me a letter asking me to come out and visit a spell. Maybe he knew that I was awful lonely there in the home in Hickory Flats. And, you remember, mother and father have more kids than chickens, so I came by train to Atlanta about three months ago. Of course, that was before the war ever reached here. I told Aunt Pauletta that I would stay here in Atlanta until fall if it was all right. I needed something to do, and I decided to begin volunteering here at the hospital about three weeks ago."

David stood listening with his mouth open in amazement.

"I never expected to see you here or really anywhere again, since you never answered my letter," she repeated, gazing into his eyes.

"Lillie, this must be a dream. How could this possibly happen — that we could meet again at a place like this?" David asked, wanting to reach over and touch her beautiful hair.

Lillie dropped her arms from around David's shoulders and took his hands in hers.

"David, it's simple," she said. "It was God who brought us back together. Maybe it was because we didn't give up on him in our disappointment."

As he looked at the beautiful Lillie, David thought, I guess you never gave up — don't know about me. I reckon God didn't give up on me though. God, please don't let this be a dream, he thought. I can't wake up in the hospital or on the battlefield to find that I've been dreaming.

She was looking into his blue eyes. As he reached for Lillie, David thought about Lum's words: "God does bless us, even though we don't deserve it."

"Lillie, can I kiss you?" David said, looking down into her beautiful face.

"Please kiss me, David," Lillie answered, with tears in her eyes.

No doubt, the long, hungry kiss made them both forget about the lonely days and nights that the lovers had longed for each other.

"David," Lillie said, stepping back and gazing into his eyes. "The Lord really blesses sometimes."

He listened as he continued to search her beautiful eyes.

"Yes, Lum — God really does bless us," Lille heard David softly say, just before he lowered his mouth again on her moist, red lips.

The End

David Riley Lofland

David R. Lofland was a great uncle to the writer, Joe Poindexter. While the story is fiction, it is based on history. David joined the Confederate army in February 20, 1862, at Danville, Arkansas. He trained at Sulfur Springs and was captured when Fort Hindman fell on January 11, 1863. He served as a prisoner of war at Camp Douglas, near Chicago, and he was released in a prisoner exchange program on April 10, 1863, at City Point, Virginia. He went back to serve in the Confederate army in Tennessee. He was wounded near Dalton, Georgia, on July 22, 1864. He survived the Civil War and eventually moved to Rockwell, Texas, where he lived until 1924. Copies of David Lofland's Confederate muster sheets are shown on the following pages.

24   Ark.

D R Lofland

Pvt , Co. I , 24 Reg't Arkansas Infantry.

Appears on

Company Muster Roll .

of the organization named above,

for July & Aug , 1862

Enlisted :

When Febry 20 , 1862

Where Danville

By whom Geo Hott

Period 3 year

Last paid :

By whom Capt Moon

To what time June 30 , 1862

Present or absent Present

Remarks : Detached as teamster

Book mark :

R Kruesi
Copyst.

---

24   Ark.

D R Lofland

Pvt , Co. I , 24 Reg't Arkansas Infantry.

Appears on

Company Muster Roll

of the organization named above,

for Aug 31/62 to April 30 186 3

Enlisted :

When Febry 20 , 1862

Where Danville

By whom Geo M Scott

Period 3

Last paid :

By whom W B Raglord

To what time Aug 31 , 1862

Present or absent Present

Remarks :

Book mark :

R Kruesi
Copyst.

ii

Confederate.

2-4   Ark.

D R Lofland

Pvt   I   Co. I 24 Regt Arkansas Infantry.

Appears on

Company Muster Roll

of the organization named above,

for   Oct 31 to Dec 31 , 1862.

Enlisted:

When   Febry 20 , 1862.

Where   Yell Co

By whom   Geo Hall

Period   3 years

Last paid:

By whom

To what time   Oct 31 , 1862

Present or absent   Present

Remarks:

Book mark:

Confederate.

2-4   Ark.

D R Lofland

Pvt   I   Co. I 24 Arkansas Infantry.

Appears on

Roll of Prisoners of War

paid at or near Camp ..... Ills., April 8, 1863, of prisoners of war, Post, Va., April 10, 1863.

Roll dated   Not dated

When captured   Arkansas Post

When captured   Jany 11 , 1863

Remarks:

Roll bears ......

Number of roll

842 : sheet

(830b)

iv